Rodeo Road Code

By Howard Pitzen

First Edition
May, 1998

Copyright © 1998, STAMPEDE PRESS
All rights reserved.

This is a work of fiction. The events described are imaginary and the characters are fictitious and not intended to represent specific persons. Even when settings are referred to by their real names, the incidents portrayed there are entirely fictitious. The reader should not infer that the events ever actually happened.

No part of this book may be reproduced by any means
without written consent of the publisher except
for brief quotes used in reviews written specifically
for use in a magazine or newspaper.

Library of Congress Cataloging in Publication Data
98-090334

ISBN 0-9664225-0-3

PRINTED IN THE UNITED STATES OF AMERICA
BY
ARROW PRINTING
Bemidji, Minnesota

Dedicated to

All the cowboys who went down the road and DIDN'T win a championship.

INTRODUCTION

The Code of the West is more or less and unwritten code, so it is paradoxel that man should be trying to put it in print, "But fools rush in where angels fear to tread."

In the early days of the west when most men packed a gun, the code was fairly simple. You didn't shoot a man in the back, you gave him fair warning. You treated a woman with respect, whether they deserved it or not. You didn't steal. You didn't cheat. You didn't lie. If a friend got into trouble, you helped him out, and didn't ask questions. You didn't ask a man where he was from, if he wants you to know he'll tell you. If a man came to your camp, you shared whatever you had. As the west settled up the code changed some but the basics remained pretty much the same. I saw a plaque once that said:

CODE OF THE COW COUNTRY

It don't take such a lot o'laws to keep the rangeland straight Nor books to write'em in, 'cause there are only six or eight

The first one is the Welcome Sign, written deep in Western Hearts My camp is yours and yours is mine in all cow country parts, Treat with respect all womankind, same as you would your sister

Care for neighbors' strays you find, and don't call cowboys 'Mister'

Shut the pasture gates when passin' through, an' taking all in all

Be just as rough as pleases you, but never mean nor small

Talk straight, shoot straight, never break your word to man nor boss

Plumb always kill a rattlesnake; don't ride a sore-back hoss

It don't take law or pedigree to live the best you can

These few is all it takes to be a cowboy an' - a man!

The code has evolved into the world of rodeo where cowboys will help each other out, even though they are complete strangers. It explains a little of why a man back east locks his car, but a rodeo contestant will lend his to a complete stranger to get to another rodeo. They call it CAMARADERIE.

But not every westerner lives up to the code any more than every Christian lives up to the ten Commandments. There were the cold-blooded killers and scoundrels, liars, thieves and cheats, then as now.

Yet it is a code to live by. As we go down the pathway of life, things are seldom the way we expect and almost never the way we want them. Life is like a big poker game and we aren't all dealt the same hand. Some of us get aces and some get eights; yet it isn't the hand we get, but how we play it that counts. And there are things that happen that can turn our lives around in an instant, for better or worse. An accident or whatever. Some people call this luck but there is really no such thing as luck. All things are ordained by God and although we don't understand most of these reasons, that doesn't change the basic truth.

Most of us don't play the game very well. We throw away aces when we should stand pat and probably throw in when we should have asked for a few. However, life is like that. As we look around us, some people seem to lose no matter what they do or how hard they try. And some seem to have it all no matter how evil or crooked. But life is like that, too. In real life, people get away with murder, theft, and all kinds of evil. Real life isn't like the T.V. shows where the mystery is always neatly wrapped up in 30 minutes with time out for commercials. Real life gets mixed up, messed up and real hard to explain.

I heard a rodeo announcer once say, "Why do cowboys do what they do? I don't know the answer to that but I do know one thing. Now, not everyone who gets exposed to rodeo gets bit by the 'rodeo bug' but those that do and get infected with the virus will never be the same again for the rest of their lives. It will get in your blood stream, it will seep into the very marrow of your bones, it will ooze out of every pore in your body. It will give you the chills when it's 100 above and it will make you sweat when it's 40 below. It will beat, bruise, batter your body and rob you of your common sense and good judgement. But for all of that, she is a Jezebel and you will love her just the same."

Buck Compton chose the rodeo road with all its tragedies and triumphs. He was like a lot of us. He didn't always play his cards right either. Life is like that too. So why don't you come along. Grab your warbag, suitcase, bedroll or whatever you are traveling with and throw it in the trunk of the car, the back of the pick-up, or in the sleeper of an eighteen wheeler, whatever Buck is traveling in at the time.

And whether you are still waiting to see your first rodeo or you are an aficionado of the great American sport, you will enjoy the trip. Just remember the Code of the West and you'll get along fine.

CHAPTER 1

I was sitting on the water truck, watching the flow of water into the stock tank as she walked by. Well, it wasn't really a water truck, it was a fire truck of the Wood River Volunteer Fire Department. Used for road fires with a holding tank of 11,000 gallon capacity. I was backed up to the arena fence and idly watching the stream of water fill the tank. At first, most of the bucking stock had crowded around, but now most of them had slacked their thirst and only those on the low end of the pecking order were drinking.

The truck was pointed north and I was sitting on top on the east side so I didn't see her 'til she passed the front of the truck headed east. I didn't get a look at her face at all. She was dressed in white that could have been a uniform although a little snug fittin'. But then if I were a woman with a figure like that, I would probably wear my clothes a little snug too. She had coal black wavy hair that set off the white uniform. Or maybe the white uniform set off the black hair.

It was still pretty early in the morning and I kind of wondered what anyone was doing out at the rodeo grounds this early, much less a woman. Not that there aren't plenty of girls who come to hang around rodeo. There are the usual 'buckle bunnies' and camp followers who come to make up part of the scenery. And then there are always some locals who are out looking for a cowboy to add to whatever kind of roster these women keep. But it was a little early for these sort of people to make the scene.

She kept walking 'til she had almost reached the end of the arena and on an impulse I yelled, "Pardon me ma'am, but you dropped your handkerchief." I didn't know if she would even hear me or if she would know I was hollering at her, or if she would ignore me. Even if she did I thought, "What the hell have I got to lose?" However, she immediately stopped and spun around to face me and snapped out, "Cotton or silk?" We both knew there was no handkerchief but apparently she was willing to go along with the little gag, and the answer stumped me for a moment. Then I remembered going to a stage show once when I was a kid and seeing the magician doing tricks, many of which were pulling big silk scarves and handkerchiefs from out of nowhere and making them disappear again. I guess the reason they use silk is because you can crush them up into almost nothing and tuck them away here and there or whatever. So I replied, "It must be silk because it disappeared."

With that she laughed, revealing a set of white, even teeth. She started to walk back slowly toward me. At 200 feet she was beautiful. At 100 feet she was still damned good-looking, but when she got up close I could see the hard lines around her eyes and mouth and the mileage in her eyes. Still, she wasn't hard to look at, and she had a figure that would make most women jealous. I guessed her to be in her mid thirties but it was hard to tell.

She walked up to the truck and asked, "What are you doing?" Since it was pretty obvious what I was doing, it was apparent that she wanted to make conversation. So I replied, "Watering and feeding the stock." Then she started asking the questions that I had heard hundreds of times before, usually by kids but sometimes by little old ladies, rarely by men. I guess the men didn't want to let on that they didn't know.

"Are these animals mean?"

"Are they trained to buck?"

"Do you torment the animals?"

"Does that strap you put around them make them buck?"

I had gotten to where I answered the questions kind of automatically without really thinking, yet tried to be polite. After all, it was good for P.R.

"No, most of them are not mean but some of them are."

"No we don't train them to buck, they buck because they want to."

"No we do not torment the animals. On the contrary, we treat them very well."

"No, the bucking strap does not make them buck. It does make a bucking animal better but if that was all it took, anyone could go out and buy an armful of flank straps and a load of "canners" and be in the stock contracting business."

Well for once I didn't mind answering the questions. In fact, I elaborated on the answers. I explained that the animals all had individual personalities, some mean and some rather docile, but they all had one thing in common or they wouldn't be here. They all wanted to buck. Real bad. Or they wouldn't stay with it.

She had seen a couple of rodeos on T.V. and wasn't real rodeo orientated. But she was company and I wasn't adverse to that. She also asked, "Do you ride?" I smiled as I answered, "No. I used to but I'm getting a little old for that."

We had talked for awhile after the tank was full and I still had to feed so I finally said, "Well I have to get the truck back to the station." Then again, on impulse, I asked, "Do you want to ride along?" and was a bit surprised when she said, "Sure." I wasn't sure what the rules and regs were concerning civilians riding the fire trucks but I figured it was early enough so that none of the big wheels were going to be around anyway.

The Wood River Lions Club put on the rodeo and they were a pretty good bunch of fellows to deal with as rodeo committees go. Every town had a little different setup as far as taking care of the stock was concerned but Doc Steen, my boss, wrote out his contracts to where the committee had to furnish the feed and the water. Some places were real good about it and would have feed and water on hand or someone there to get whatever you needed. Some places were bad and you almost had to wonder if you hit the right town. When you arrived you would have to hunt up someone to find the feed and water and no one seemed to know who was in charge. Usually these places didn't last. They either got their act together or the rodeo folded.

At Wood River we kept the stock in the arena with a portable stock tank just inside the fence. The Fire Dept. loaned us the truck to haul water to the stock. Some places had piped-in water but at most rodeos, we had to get it hauled one way or the other. In most of the smaller towns, there is usually about the same bunch of people who belong to the Chamber of Commerce, Rotary Club, the Lions or whatever, so that there was a lot of trading as far as services go among the group. When I arrived in Wood River, the committee took me up to the fire hall and showed me the fire truck and how to use it and they gave me a set of keys. One of them showed me how to fill it up again after I brought it back, so in case of a fire it would be ready to go. I was satisfied with the arrangement.

After I got the truck back in the fire hall and parked, I turned on the valve to fill it. All this time we hadn't talked. I was still kind of wondering what her game was. We still hadn't introduced ourselves so I stuck out my hand and said "My name is Bill Compton, but everyone calls me Buck. If the outfit I was working for was bigger, I guess I would be called the livestock superintendent but usually I'm referred to as the 'flunkie'."

I tried to smile a little as I said this, kind of hoping she would get the humor but she didn't respond in kind.

"Just call me Sandy," she said as she shook my hand. She had a firm handshake and I liked that. Even in a woman. She didn't offer any more conversation and sat down on a worn chair by the wall.

I was watching her when I heard water gushing and saw the tank running over. I rushed over and turned off the valve. No harm was done as the truck was parked by a floor drain, but it gave me an excuse to say something.

"Rule number one: Pay attention to what you're doing." She laughed a little at that one.

We left the fire hall and walked over to where I had parked the boss's pick-up to drive back to the rodeo grounds. It was a year-old Dodge Club Cab dually with a fifth wheel hook-up that hauled the gear wagon. This was a big gooseneck trailer that we packed all the rodeo gear into with room in the back for any extra stock that needed hauling. Usually I carried the pick up horses and a few extras. There was a compartment over the hookups, which I made into a sleeper, that was kind of my home away from home. Well, actually it was my home because I really didn't have a home anymore. Unless you could call the bunkhouse at the boss's home ranch a home. But I spent very little time there anyway, although I did leave some odds and ends there for storage.

Now that fire truck was pretty clean and I hadn't thought much about it when Sandy had crawled in there with those white clothes on, but the pick-up that we called 'Big Red' (the boss liked red) was another story. Although it was considered 'my' truck, anybody on the payroll was apt to drive it and we used it for hauling hay, feed or anything else that needed hauling, and what with sitting in the dust, mud and manure, it just got that 'used' look.

I moved up ahead of her quick like and said, "Hold on a minute, I think I'm gonna have to do a little house cleaning first." I made room for her but the seats were stained with everything from spilled beer to tobacco juice and I didn't know how much would rub off onto those white clothes. I looked behind the seat to find my yellow slicker and draped that over the seat for her to sit on.

She jumped in and said, "Thanks!" She was game.

As I started the truck she said, "Now what?"

"Well, it's back to the rodeo grounds. I need to feed the saddle horses and then I need to feed myself. I haven't had breakfast yet. I feel kind of gant." Again on an impulse I asked, "Would you care to join me?"

She really warmed to that and said, "I would be glad to!" I grained the saddle horses and we headed uptown to a diner. We walked in and found a table. There weren't too many people around. Mostly people on their way to work.

I thought, "Damn, where are all of those cowboys now? Here I am sitting with a good-looking woman and not a damn one of them shows up to see me."

I hadn't actually expected to see anyone I knew. Most of the contestants hadn't arrived yet and those that had were sacked out someplace 'til at least mid-morning. Even the hands on the payroll slept in because 'Old Buck' looked after the feeding and watering. Then too, unlike back at the ranch, on the rodeo circuit you had a tendency to get to bed later so you got to sleep when you could. But whether there was anyone I knew around to see me or not, it sure didn't hurt my ego any to sit down to breakfast with a good-looking woman. Actually my love and social life had gotten pretty sparse in later years. Well, actually it never was too lucrative. Most people, I suppose, figure the life of a rodeo cowboy is pretty glamorous. You go out and make winning ride all dressed up in satin shirts and fringed chaps. Then as you pick up your check at the pay window, beautiful women mob you as you go off to a big party and you live it up 'til you make the next ride.

Well, that's not quite the way it is. For most of us it was a hard, grueling way of life that we endured, not even quite knowing why. There was an occasional cowboy who was loaded with talent, who kind of started winning right off, but most of us put in a few years before we got to go to the pay window very steady. There were the years of several cowboys traveling together in a beat-up car or truck, pooling expenses and hoping one of the bunch would make enough money to get us to the next rodeo. Sometimes we could get on the work list to help pay the entry fees. Sometimes we had to drop out for awhile and find a part-time job to make enough to go again. And sometimes (I hate to think about it now) we got a little help with that Arkansas credit card, a rubber hose we kept behind the seat in case of an emergency.

It really hurt when we went to those rodeos and those good looking girls smiled and gave you the high sign but down in your pocket you maybe had enough money for ONE hamburger. Well, you don't go asking for a date under those circumstances. You grit your teeth, smile back and go on about your way. Maybe today if I can fit a ride on old 'Butter Milk' and win a first, I'll look her up and we can go eat steak and maybe party a little, who knows.

But old 'Butter Milk' blew out of the chute, sucked back, and bucked to the left and somewhere off in the distance you could hear the announcer, "Well folks all he is going to get for that entry fee is your applause. What do you say we give him a hand. Old 'Butter Milk' sure turned the crank today."

Then eventually you start winning a little. Oh, not much. A fourth or a third in day money but it sure makes you feel good to get up to the pay window once in a while and it makes your hat fit a little tighter but you still don't have much money left over for the finer things in life. Now you can buy a new shirt once in a while and stop at a laundromat and wear cleaner clothes and get in on an occasional party. But even when you got to a few of the rodeo parties, there wasn't all that much to choose from. Most of the girls that hang around the grand entry gate or the bars and honky tonks in the rodeo towns were not the kind you would like to take home and introduce to your mother. Some of the cowboys just didn't give a damn, of course, and would bed down with anything. I guess they were looking for quanity not quality.

And then comes the day you start hitting your luck. You start winning on a regular basis. Until now, you didn't realize how many things there are in life that you couldn't get along without. That old bronc saddle just don't seem right all of a sudden. Never mind that it is the one you started winning in. It's just that you figure a new one would be a little better, so you order one custom made. And, of course, you need a vehicle.

Things don't change all that much. There's still a bunch of traveling together, (usually all you can cram into the rig). But now it's your rig and, hopefully, someone else is putting the gas in. It does give you more flexibility as you get to pick which rodeo you go to. But you still don't have much time to party, or for a social life.

And then you get good enough to hit the big shows. You dream about becoming a World Champion. You start rodeoing HARD. Maybe if your luck holds and you draw good, you can get to the Finals. You're winning more than you ever did before, but you use most of it up in travel expenses and entry fees. Now when you reflect on it, it ain't much different than when you started out. You are traveling in a better rig, and eating more regular, but all too often, it is still just a hot dog or hamburger on the run. You are still just getting to the next rodeo and competing, with very little time for anything else. Some of the cowboys pick up a "honey" on the way, and she travels with him a while 'til the glamour wears off, and then old home looks a lot better than it used to and she goes back to where she came from.

Occasionally, one gets married, but for the most part, it is lots of miles traveled with too little sleep. Along about here, a lot of the cowboys get 'road foundered', and they give up for a different way of life. Some kind of get back into rodeo later on in a more subdued way, but some quit her completely.

Now there are exceptions to every rule. There are those cowboys who show up at every rodeo with some real good looking chic. He is usually dressed up like Roy Rogers or Gene Autry, and usually is a bull rider. No one has ever seen him make the whistle on a bull, and in fact, it quite often turns out he has a doctor's order not to ride that day, something about his back or shoulder or leg. But, if he finally draws one he thinks he can ride, he will give it a try. Anyway, ride or not, he has his name in the program, and he usually has a program in his hip pocket. These fellows are usually pretty good looking, but not necessarily. They are more full of the fertilizer than the bull they are riding. And there definitely is a market for that kind of fertilizer. These dudes are usually traveling first class, and not on their own money. They have found some good looking honey with a big car and a checkbook, (quite often daddy's), and they live it up 'til the gal gets wise or tired of the B.S., and then they probably both move on to another.

Well, getting back to me, I was certainly not a celibate, but I was sure no libertine either. In later years, when I went to work for old Doc Steen, my encounters with the fair sex were getting few and far between. And so it felt good just to be sitting across the table from a woman and enjoying her company.

An elderly waitress came with a pot of coffee and poured us two cups without asking. And then she said, "What'll it be cowboy? The rodeo cowboys' special is steak and eggs."

I had been eating alone so much lately, that I kind of forgot my manners and instead of deferring to the woman first, I said, "I'll have the special."

Now, I have dined with more than a few women in my life, and especially in the morning, they usually skimp by on toast and coffee, or some such light thing. Especially the trim ones, but Sandy didn't hesitate a moment when she said, I'll have the same." And when the waitress brought back two platters of steak and eggs, with a huge helping of hashbrowns, she dug in like a starved puppy.

This woman was becoming more intriguing all the time. My first impression that she was some woman looking for a cowboy just didn't fit the pattern. Then the thought slowly evolved in my not-too-bright mind, that this gal was hungry. She still hadn't volunteered any information about herself.

As she finished cleaning up her plate, I casually asked, "When was the last time you ate?"

She was quiet a moment, and then said softly, "Yesterday morning, I guess", then smiled and added, "I was getting kind of gant, too."

We sat in silence awhile sipping our coffee. I was sure inquisitive about her, but I didn't want to violate the "Code of the West" by asking.

Finally, she looked me straight in the eye and said, "You don't know how much I hate to ask you this, but could you lend me $20? I'm traveling light, and there are some things I need. You can leave me here uptown and drive back by yourself. It's not that far to the rodeo grounds, and I'll walk back. The excercise will do me good."

Without replying, I slowly reached into my billfold and gave her a $20 bill. Hell, with that soulful lost look she gave me, I would have probably given her my whole paycheck. She got up then and said "See you later at the rodeo," and turned and walked out.

Well, old Buck had been suckered before by hard-luck stories and con jobs, and I thought I was getting immune to those kind of things, but if this one didn't beat all. "Well, you asked for it" I told myself. "Here she got breakfast out of you and a $20 tip besides, and you didn't even get to hold hands. She didn't even have a bad luck story. Just asked for the money, and you gave it to her. And you don't know anymore about her now than when you first saw her. Oh well, she was company to an old man.

I did have to smile, though, when I recalled her last words, "See you later at the rodeo."

I got up, paid my bill. Cowboys are notoriously poor tippers, and I am one of them, but this morning, I left a generous tip. After all, the waitress hadn't asked for a loan. I drove back to the rodeo grounds and planned on taking a couple of hours nap before the crew arrived to sort stock for the final performance this afternoon. I crawled into the sleeper and slipped off my boots. I usually don't have trouble dropping off to sleep, but I couldn't get Sandy out of my mind.

"You damned old fool," I told myself. "Forget it. You'll never see her again, and what's $20?"

I must have dozed off though, because the next thing I know, Tom McCain was banging on the sleeper saying, "Come on, Buck. Time to work stock."

CHAPTER 2

Tom was the pick-up man along with Rick Kellog. I was usually the chute boss and did the flanking. Although, we were all pretty versatile, and could fill in where needed when the occasion arose.

"Oh, by the way, Rick won't be here. He had to take off. Death in the family or something. Doc says for you to pick-up, and he will flank himself."

Doc Steen, the contractor, had about done everything in rodeo one time or another. He used to flank all his own horses, but arthritis kind of hampered his getting around. He delegated most of the jobs out in later years. Still, he could handle it and did move in when the occasion called for it.

We moved the stock out of the arena into a big "waste" pen and started sorting. Wood River had a permanent arena and a pretty good set-up. Going down the road, we worked under all kinds of conditions, and not all of them good. More and more, we used portable arenas. Then we didn't have as many pens, and sometimes we parked the trucks and trailers to make a waste pen or pens. But sometimes we didn't even have the room to do that. Still we managed to get by somehow. As I said, here at Wood River they had a good set-up.

I would cut out the horses one at a time from the waste pen. From there they ran down an alley that fronted the holding pens. We penned the horses in the order that they were on the program and put a man on the gate at each pen. I had a program with the "draw" for the last performance and as each horse came out, I would holler, "First section bares; second section bares; saddle bronc; re-rides or waste pen." We then sorted the bulls and the rest of the stock. I could hear the tractor tilling up the arena and all of the familiar sounds that I had heard millions of times before.

I had a little gasoline camp stove that I carried with me in the trailer and broke it out now and then to heat some water. I had a couple of canvas sheets as part of the gear that I hung inside to give myself a little privacy. I proceeded to take a 'bath in a bucket' and get cleaned up.

I guess to most folks, the people connected with rodeos border on celebrity status and for some this is probably true, but for most of us, we live a pretty humble life. After all, when the announcer calls your name and you ride out during the introductions all dressed up, half the people in the audience would like to trade places with you.

I usually 'roughed it' in the trailer. The little camp stove came in handy. Although I usually took my meals in a cafe or concession stand, I did keep some emergency rations stowed in the sleeper, and on occasion, would heat up a meal on the stove when I pulled in someplace where nothing was open.

I heated more water to shave with and got dressed up for the performance. I dug out a white shirt and red silk scarf. Doc always had his pick-up men in white shirts, just one of his little trademarks. Doc was a good man to work for. He had his ideas about how a show should be run and was pretty positive about it, but he was fair. The white shirts were one of them, but he picked up the cleaning bill on them and we couldn't complain about that.

As 2:00 p.m. approached, the tension started to build in the air. I had been around rodeos over 40 years now, and yet the old excitement always comes back as the Grand Entry gets ready and mounted up. During the Grand Entry we had a number of the cowboys and cowgirls carry flags. We went through a maneuver usually called the serpentine. Then it was time for introductions.

We didn't always do things the same way. Sometimes the committee had ideas of their own, but at Wood River they let Doc put on the show any way he wanted to. Doc was a kind of traditionalist. The pick-up men carried the American flag. I deferred to Tom McCain and let him carry Old Glory.

I could feel the tension building in 'Roany', my pick-up horse. He had been through this hundreds of times, and he could feel the same excitement as the cowboys.

And then I heard the announcer say, "And filling in for Rick Kellog, who is unable to be here this afternoon, is your other pick-up man bearing the flag of the M.D. Rodeo Co., Buck Compton of Bad River, South Dakota."

I touched my spurs to Roany, and we exploded into the arena with the wind whipping the rodeo flag as we circled the arena. As I rode through the entry gate, a girl wearing a long flowing dress, a big brimmed straw hat, not a western hat, but the kind you see women tending flowers wear, and dark glasses was standing off to the side. She waved at me as I galloped through the gate. I thought she looked vaguely familiar, but couldn't quite place her and didn't have time to dwell on it.

As I rode around the arena, I came to a halt beside Tom holding the American flag. I stole a glance back at the entry gate but didn't see her. As the National Anthem played, my thoughts turned to the coming performance. Most of the horses would be pretty easy to pick-up, but there were a couple that would be tough, and we had to concentrate on those.

Eventually it was over, and now we could relax some. The announcer thanked everyone for coming and hoped to see them all again next year, etc. The crowd drifted away. Most of the contestants were leaving, too. Some of them gathered in bunches and talked over the rodeo or where they were going or had been. There was no beer stand at Wood River, but coolers came out, and anyone who wanted a cool one didn't have a problem finding one. Tom always had some on ice, and although I wasn't a drinking man, a cool beer would taste pretty good about now.

When he offered me one, I didn't refuse.

I was unsaddling my horse by the gear trailer when I heard a familiar voice behind me say, "I thought you said you didn't ride."

I spun around, and there she stood smiling.

"No wonder I didn't recognize you," I said, "with that long dress and hat." She had taken the dark glasses off. "Oh, about riding, let me explain. Around rodeo, when someone says he rides, that means the rough stock. He is competing. It doesn't mean riding saddle horses." I laughed, "I'll most likely be riding these critters 'til I can't get on anymore."

"But where did you get those clothes, don't tell me you did all that on $20."

I was kind of tingly all over. When I last saw her this morning, I didn't think I'd ever see her again, and what with all the activities and excitement, I plumb forgot all about her. Then suddenly, here she was again from out of nowhere it seemed.

Suddenly I was feeling kind of macho, and said, "Look, I haven't really eaten since breakfast and I'm getting kind of gant again, would you join me for supper?"

When she said, "Sure," again, I felt ten years younger. I was old enough to be her dad but suddenly I wasn't tired anymore.

I said, "First I have to feed the stock and then I'll be right with you."

The man from the fire department had brought the truck out and was filling the tank. Doc made arrangements to leave the stock over night and we would load out in the morning. I hollered at a couple of the boys on the work list and we took 'Big Red' to the bale stack and loaded up the rest of the hay. The stock had been turned into the arena and were fighting for a place at the stock tank. As one of the boys drove, the other dumped bales off in big circles in the arena. As they pulled up with the empty truck, I said "Thanks boys."

I shook out that slicker again and opened the door for Sandy to get in. I could see the remaining cowboys casting sideways glances at us as we drove off for uptown. After we were out of ear shot the talk would be, "Hey, Bucks' got a girlfriend and a looker, too! What do you know about that? Didn't think he had it in him."

Like I said, this wasn't hurting my ego a damn bit.

Still I couldn't quite figure this thing out. She definitely wasn't some gal out lookin for a cowboy. Or was she? Maybe she just ran into old Buck this morning when she was hungry and would be looking over the crop during the performance and not getting connected, came back to her meal ticket. No, it just didn't fit. The hustlers come the first day of the rodeo, not the last. And they were around the night crowd, not out early in the morning. And even the gals out looking for the cowboys, they didn't all end up with a contestant but there were plenty of unattached men around, ranch hands and working cowboys from the surrounding area in for the rodeo. Maybe back east, but not usually out west, would a gal on the make be left alone by rodeo's end.

But I didn't say anything on the ride uptown. I had plenty of time and was in no hurry even though I was damn inquisitive. Strange, when you get older and there is little left to life, you have lots of time. When you are young and your whole life is ahead of you, you don't seem to have any.

We drove to the edge of town where there was a supper club. I thought, what the hell, might as well live it up a little. I wasn't really dressed for this place but it was still early and it was rodeo week. I still had the white shirt on that I wore during the perf and it showed the effects of the dirt and the sweat. And I still had on my silk scarf so that qualified for the "TIES REQUIRED" sign.

As it turned out, a couple of the committee men were there with their wives and nodded towards me. One came over to comment on the good rodeo and the good job I did as pick-up man. I thanked him but believed he was more or less doing P.R. work.

Sandy looked great in the dress that she had on. The top looked like a blouse and was white with lace around the edges. The bottom was blue and came down about halfway between her knees and ankles. A belt around the middle gave the impression that it was a blouse and a skirt. She carried the big straw hat which gave her a kind of dressed-up peasant look.

We found a corner table and eventually I ordered steak and she ordered a big salad.

"Wow!" I said, "Tell me how you managed that wardrobe on $20." She laughed and said, "It didn't cost me anything. When I left you, I went to a phone booth. I looked up and found there was a Salvation Army store in town and a number to call in case of an emergency. I knew the store wouldn't be open on Sunday so I called the number. A woman answered. I told her there wasn't exactly an emergency but it was real close and that I really did need some clothes. The dear old soul told me to meet her at the store and she outfitted me in this dress. I also got some other clothes and a bag to carry them in."

"Don't tell me you still have the $20?"

"No. I had to buy a ticket to get back into the rodeo."

"Darn, why didn't I think of that? I could have got a pass for you. Well, a little late for that now."

We talked about a number of things, like the rodeo, etc. but nothing very serious. By the time we left the supper club, it was dark. We got into 'Big Red' and sat there a while in silence. I wondered if she was available, and 20 or 30 years ago, I would have found out. But not having any children of my own, I was kind of getting to feel like a father to her and feeling protective. Maybe I didn't want to find out. Strange. Finally, I broke the silence, "What now?"

"This may sound kind of strange, but could I sleep in the pick-up tonight? I really don't have any other place to go."

I thought I was prepared for anything, but that one threw me. I guess I could have, in fact should have, asked why and a whole bunch of other questions but I didn't. I just put the pick-up in gear and headed for the rodeo grounds. It was quiet out there now. In fact, there is nothing as quiet as a rodeo grounds after a rodeo is over. Even the stock seem to know that it is over for a while and time to kick back and relax.

I pulled up beside the trailer and said, "Look, this is no place for a woman to sleep. Let me clean up the sleeper a little bit and you can have my bed. There are plenty of blankets, seein' as how I carry enough for cold weather. I'll take a couple of blankets and a tarp and make my bed over by the hay stack."

I think she was going to argue with me but finally said simply, "You are very kind."

I straightened things out the best I could in the sleeper and took extra gear to the hay stack, what was left of it. I managed to scatter out enough to make a reasonable mattress and put the tarp and blankets down and crawled in. It was a bright, cloudless night but no moon and the Milky Way was lit up like no carnival I had ever seen.

I didn't think I would ever get to sleep. I couldn't help but wonder what the 'copy' was on Sandy. (If that was her real name.) She was running from something, but I had no way of knowing what. She was too old for your normal runaway girl. Maybe she was like the hippies searching for themselves, but that didn't fit either. And why pick on Old Buck? Maybe she felt secure and safe with me. I smiled to myself a little at that. She didn't know what kind of sinner Old Buck was. I supposed that eventually she would tell me about herself and I was in no real hurry, I guess.

In the meantime I wondered about tomorrow. I must have dropped off sometime before morning because I suddenly woke up and the sun was shining. I got up quickly and folded the blankets. I hustled over to the trailer but Sandy was already up and dressed in a shirt and denim jeans.

She smiled and said, "I got these from the Salvation Army store, too. I zonked right out last night, first real good night's sleep I have had in a long time. Thanks for the bedroom."

I am usually an early riser, except when I have been driving all night but now I was anxious to get going, as I had slept later than usual. The plan was that I was to take the gooseneck with the gear and 'using' horses to Roundsville, about 200 milies away. Floyd Gilham was going to be there with the chutes, from the home ranch, about 150 miles on the other side of Roundsville. Roundsville was going to be a County Fair rodeo on Friday and Saturday evenings. They had a great grandstand but no permanent arena. Floyd would meet me there and we would set up the arena so we could dump the stock and then the whole crew would set up the chutes and pens.

In years past, any place that wanted to put on a rodeo usually built an arena, but in later years a lot of rodeos were hosted in places where the grandstand or stadium is used for other things throughout the year. Almost every stock contractor had a set of portable chutes and panels to make up an arena and holding pens.

We had loaded the trailer with the gear last night and I went to get the horses. Sandy walked along with me. As I was putting halters on the horses, Sandy asked where I was going. I told her briefly what the schedule was but wasn't prepared for what came next. I just kind of figured I would be moving on and she would be a nice but brief memory.

"Can I go along?" She asked simply. I stopped dead in my tracks and after a brief and awkward silence she asked again, "Don't you want me along?"

"Well it isn't that I don't want you along. In fact, I would be glad to have the company you are, well, I don't know what Doc would think, or, well I just don't know. I'll think about it."

To hurry things along, I gave her two of the horses to lead to the trailer. Doc was waiting by the trailer. He gave Sandy a sideways glance as she stood back with the two horses.

"There has been a change of plans, "Doc said, as he appeared kind of agitated. I figured he probably didn't care too much about me taking up with a woman, but that wasn't his concern at the moment.

"Floyd is down with some kind of flu and can't drive. Could you drive to Roundsville, unhook the trailer, go to the ranch and pick up the chutes? We'll have to have somebody go back after the pick-up."

I always kind of liked that about Doc. He never really told you to do something, he always asked you to. 'Course you knew if you wanted to stay on the payroll, you damn sure better, but it was still nice to be asked anyway. "I'll hold the stock here 'til this evening. Rick and Tom will help you set up when they get there. I hate to have the stock sit on the truck while you fellows are setting up, but hauling in the evening when it's cooler will help and I'll be done with my business here and will be there to help what I can."

Sandy had stood back and took all this in. It didn't take much of a mathematician to figure out there was going to be some hard driving, about 500 miles and then some dead heading back to get the pick-up. She stepped up to Doc and said, "I could go along and drive the pick-up back. That would help some."

"Oh, by the way Doc, this is Sandy. Sandy, this Doc Steen, owner of this outfit."

She stepped up and they shook hands and I knew he would be impressed with that firm handshake. He hesitated only a moment and then he looked at me and said, "Whatever you think" and turned and walked away.

It was not a time to be too fussy. We had a show to put on and the show must go on. Many a clown or rodeo announcer got his start by just being in the right spot at the right time, when some clown or announcer failed to make the connection.

"Let's go," I said, and we loaded up and took off. We didn't have time for the luxury of a breakfast so as I pulled up to a truck stop on the edge of town to fill up the fuel tanks, I told Sandy to grab us some coffee and whatever she could find to eat on the way.

"There's a thermos behind the seat." I yelled as I jumped out.

I filled the tank and went in to settle up and Sandy had a slip at the counter for the lunch. I settled up and we were on our way.

First, she broke out two bottles of orange juice. "Got to have our vitamin C," she said. After that we drove in silence as I did a balancing act with my driving, and eating.

It was beginning to warm up so I rolled down the window. 'Big Red' didn't have 'air'. The wind rushing through the cab made conversation a little difficult and anyway, I was pushing it and watching for 'smokies'. We made it to Roundsville in a little over four hours. We had made good time so far.

I unhooked the trailer, unloaded the horses and found a pen behind one of the barns with grass in it and turned them loose. We topped off the fuel tank at another truck stop and took on some more coffee and sandwiches.

I said, "You might as well start getting acquainted with this rig. Have you ever drove a pick-up before?"

"I drove several different cars and a van. I think I can handle this." She jumped in and took off like a trooper while I read the map and acted like a navigator.

The first 100 miles were good road but the last 50 were into the foothills and the last 10 were a dirt road into the ranch. I let her drive the first 100 miles and then took over as I had been there more than a few times myself and I knew how fast you could take the corners and curves. I was going to have to take it pretty slow with the tractor and trailer and Sandy wouldn't have any trouble keeping up to me coming back out.

When we got to the ranch, things looked awful quiet. The rig was sitting there. I checked the fuel tanks and oil and everything was ready to go.

I went to the bunkhouse and opened the door. The shades were all pulled and it was quite dark in there. It took me a minute to adjust my eyes.

"Floyd?" I asked. A weak voice answered from the corner bunk. "You ok, Floyd?" I asked as I moved closer.

"I think I'll make it."

I was torn between taking care of my fellow man and catching the same bug he had. He had a bucket beside the bunk and the foul odor from it drifted over to me.

"I'll be all right." He said. "I just figured I was too weak to pilot the truck into Roundsville. Afraid I might pile her up. Rodreguz is looking after me. Went into town for some medicine."

Rodreguz was the only other man on the place when we were out rodeoing and in fact the only man when Floyd was gone. Floyd was kind of a handy man, truck driver, etc., and could sit on a horse when we worked stock but wasn't much of a cowboy. Rodreguz was an ancient Mexican that Doc had inherited when he bought the ranch. No one seemed to know how old he was. He did chores, kept a garden, did the cooking when he had to and could also sit a horse. He had got to where he needed help to get aboard but once up, he seemed right at home. He didn't hardly ever move fast either on foot or horseback but always seemed to know where to be at the right time to save a lot of steps and a lot of riding.

Doc had an old pick-up that was left at the ranch and apparently Rodreguz or Rod as the boys called him, had taken that to town. I figured that everything was under control and there wasn't much of anything I could do anyway so I climbed behind the wheel in the semi and proceeded to navigate the curves and hills until we got to the blacktop.

It was just getting dark when I could see the water tower of Roundsville up ahead. As I pulled into the fairgrounds, I saw a sight to gladden my heart. The flood lights were turned on and Doc's station wagon was parked by the grandstand. He had hurried up his business at Wood River and then high balled over to Roundsville. He hunted up someone from the fairboard and got the combination to the lights and had the water turned on and a tank filling. He also managed to scrounge up a couple of helpers.

And Marge, Doc's wife, had anticipated that we had been on the run all day with not much time for eating. She had a regular buffet set out for us. Sandwiches, coffee and lemonade, potato salad and rolls.

As I came up to the spread I said, "Marge, I would hug you if Doc wasn't so close."

We did a lot of joking. Actually she was a real sweetheart. She kept Doc's books and was a real asset to the operation. Doc could be pretty caustic at times and I know there were different times when some of the help would be ready to quit, that Marge would have a talk with them and smooth things over. I didn't think that Doc knew about most of those deals.

Doc and Marge didn't have any sons. They had one daughter who had become a teacher and didn't seem too interested in rodeos or ranching. I think this hurt old Doc and Marge as it seems to be every rancher's and farmer's desire to have a son to pass on the farm or ranch to. To Marge, it seemed like all of the hands were all of her sons no matter how much of a rounder they were. We had some pretty tough hands around on occasion and Marge talked to all of them the same way and they sure respected her. If she had told the toughest one to wash behind his ears, he would have obeyed her. Anyway, we worked down a feed and commenced setting up the panels for the arena.

With the extra help, it really didn't take that long. There was a dirt track in front of the grandstand. We set up so the chutes would be facing the grandstand with all the holding pens in the infield.

Sandy dug in with the rest and was a worker. We got set up and even had time for another cup of coffee before the stock rolled in. There was still a lot of work to do tomorrow but the main part was done to contain the stock for tonight. All we had left to do was feed and Doc had put the two extra hands to loading up Big Red.

"I'm glad the stock won't have to stand in the truck." Doc commented. That would be Doc, always thinking about the stock first.

It wasn't long before Rick and Tom came in with the pots. Rick, Tom, and I were the only steady hands that went with the outfit. We all had truck driver licenses and were versatile, but mostly I flanked and was chute boss. Rick and Tom were pick-up men. All the other men were on a work list on a piece-meal basis. Sometimes Doc would hire an act or rodeo clown for the season, but sometimes he hired several here and there. Some shows, the committees hired those personnel. Anyway it was a small, compact and efficient operation.

CHAPTER 3

When the stock was unloaded and cared for, it was past midnight. A good hot shower would have felt good but no one had made provisions for that. Anyway we were so tired that we all 'crashed' and slept 'til dawn. We all got up after sunrise and went uptown for breakfast in Big Red. I introduced Sandy to Rick and Tom as we all piled into the cab with Sandy sitting on Tom's lap. For a moment I felt a twinge of jealousy. I thought, "Hey, are you getting emotionally involved here?" I tried to convince myself that I wasn't and let it go at that.

At breakfast we discussed how we would set up the rest of the arena. I would contact the fair secretary and get the front end loader down there to unload the chutes still on the flat-bed trailer. I expect we were kind of a motley-looking crew there that morning, but time to clean up later.

We had everything pretty well set up by noon. Rick and Tom had gotten a motel room and cleaned up. Sandy and I also went up to their room to use their facilities to clean up and change clothes. Rick and Tom went outside and were sitting on the step. I told Sandy to go ahead and clean up first while I waited outside too.

Rick was the younger of the two. I think twenty-five at the time and still single. He was freckle-faced with curly red hair and always seemed to have a mischievous look about him. He was, in fact, mischievous and not above playing a prank on you on occasion. We got along well together and quite often joshed and joked one another.

When Sandy went in alone, Rick cocked his eye up at me and asked, "Aren't you going to scrub her back?"

"Sorry Rick, this one's just a friend."

He was about to say something, some risque joke perhaps, but saw the look on my face and decided to remain silent.

Tom was about ten years older and married. He had a small ranch in Utah where his wife held down the spread and had a part-time job in town. They had two boys who were making hands. They got to a rodeo we worked, on occasion, if it was not too far from home. Tom was quiet and reserved. He was a hell of a cowboy and dreamed of the day he could prove up on the ranch and stay home.

After we cleaned up, I offered to buy dinner for the 'use of the room' and we were a much more presentable looking bunch when we went uptown the second time. Although Doc never said so in so many words, I knew he trusted his crew to put on a good front. It really wasn't hard to do. Doc's M.D. Rodeo Co. was a good outfit, and we all felt we were 'riding for the brand'.

The pressure was off now for a couple of days although there was always something to do. I used the afternoon to clean out the stock trailer and air out the bedding. The weather was hot so we went up and did all the laundry and took it back to the fairgrounds to hang out all day.

For supper, we went to the supermarket and bought some fruit and vegetables and made up a salad and some sandwiches and picnicked out at the grounds. The stock had been fed, and watering was easy, as they had a hose running out to the stock tank. All I had to do was turn it on and off.

The day was winding down. It had been hot but as the sun was setting, it started cooling off. We were sitting on a grassy dirt bank watching the sun set. When we were busy it was nice to have her around but now the silence crept in and neither of us spoke for some time.

Suddenly she asked, still looking at the sunset, "Were you ever in love?"

She had a way of kind of keeping one off balance. How come she never asked if I had ever been married or about my family or whatever? But instead she comes out with, "Have you ever been in love?"

I was silent a long time and I think she thought I hadn't heard her when she turned to me and was about to ask again.

"Yes I was. Once. About thirty years ago. Strange. Her name is almost like yours. Cindy. She was blond and blue eyed."

"Did you marry her?"

"No I never married. I was about twenty-five and really starting to hit a hot lick. It was at a rodeo in North Dakota in the spring. I was going to go all out and really show the world what a bronc rider could do. I drew a big stout bucking horse called 'Big John'. He was a good horse but a little hard to get out on. He would fight the chutes and you had to handle him with kid gloves. When he came out, he would rear way up. Well the day I had him, he reared up and instead of plunging out to the left, he threw his head to the right. I rode with my right hand on the buck rein and I pulled his head around more toward me to keep from falling off his back. This threw him off balance and he fell out of the chute on his left side. I didn't get away from the wreck in time and ended up with a broken left leg. Well, there was nothing to do but go home and heal up.

"I was sitting in the kitchen with my leg in a cast drinking coffee and feeling mighty blue and sorry for myself when I heard the screen door slam. I thought it was mother because no one knocked. She breezed in with a bouncy kind of walk and started right off with, 'Well how's our big hero getting along?' She was real irritating. She was obviously not impressed with my legendary bronc ride. It's funny, I had a little trouble placing her at first. She lived down the road a piece and was five years younger than I was. I finally remembered the thin little girl in braids who came around the rodeo on occasion and who showed up at the brandings. She and some of the other girls were forever pulling pranks on us "older cowboys."

"One I remember in particular. We were at a branding. I was fourteen and she would have been nine. Darwin Johnson, Gordon Runedahul and myself kind of chummed together. The crew, mostly neighbors, had brought the herd in and the men were getting the cattle to settle down and mother up. The men were taking a break and having a beer or some coffee. Darwin's mom was a terrific cook and had made up a batch of donuts. The women would be bringing dinner out later but the men had brought lunch along with the trucks. Branding was a family and neighborhood affair. The neighbors all pitched in and helped each other. Most of us would get wrapped up in it. The whole family usually came out, kids and all.

"Anyway, Darwin had snitched a sack of those donuts and hid them under a bush away from the corral. That little excursion hadn't gone unnoticed however. When we took the break, us three guys headed for that sack of donuts. As we got near the spot, my mouth was already watering from saliva at the thought of having that stash all to ourselves. When Darwin opened the sack, I caught the odor, but Darwin was so intent that he had already plunged his hand into the sack of horse manure.

"Darwin only had time to say, 'what the,' when we heard the giggles.

"Off to one side in a little dip were several small girls lying in the grass. If we hadn't been so intent on those donuts, we would have seen them before, but they had gone unnoticed 'til now. We all looked at them and our jaws dropped. Then they burst out laughing. I remember Cindy laughing and rolling in the grass, so hard, the tears ran down her cheeks.

"She was no longer the little girl in pigtails. She had grown up in the meantime. She was no longer a tomboy kid but a young woman. And in spite of her irritating ways, a damned good looking one at that. Which made it all the more irritating."

'Why aren't you out helping your dad? He's fixing the mower,' Cindy quipped.

"Aw, I do have a broken leg you know."

"Well you have crutches don't you? You going to sit there 'til you die of old age? I bet you make it in here at meal times." With that she spun around and went out and I heard the screen door slam again.

"Boy could she get under your skin. I sure was not going to get any sympathy there. But as I thought about it she WAS right. Although I wasn't going to tell her that. I gradually hobbled out to help my dad.

"I found that in weeks to come, I could do a lot to help out. I drove the old pick-up in to town for parts and supplies. I learned to drive with my right foot. When I had to step on the clutch and brake at the same time, I rigged up a stick I could push the clutch down with. I also drove the tractor during haying time. All during this time Cindy kept coming around, bugging me it seemed, but she also helped me out a lot. Dad had bought a big round baler so that he could pretty well put up hay alone if he had to, but Cindy's folks still put up hay with square bales. She had a brother at home yet and her dad hired a hand during the summer. I offered too, and was accepted to drive tractor on the baler. Cindy and her kid brother would stack bales on the hay wagon towed by the baler. That gal may have looked kind of fragile but the way she could stack bales would make a lot of men cringe.

"Anyways the summer was progressing and we were seeing more of each other. It got to where she was bothering me more than irritating me and we played jokes and pranks on each other 'til one day when we came in from haying on a hot afternoon at her folks place. They had a big round stock tank that had a spring pipe running water into it. We were hot and dry so we went over to the tank for a drink. There was a tin cup hanging on a fence post. I took the cup and let it fill from the pipe and downed the first cup and filled it again. Cindy didn't wait for the cup but bent over the edge of the stock tank to drink from the end of the pipe. She was wearing a long sleeve blue chambray shirt and it was wet on her back from the sweat and sticking to her back. I looked at her back bent over and couldn't resist the temptation. I threw the cup of cold water right on the wet spot on her back. I had expected her to throw up her hands and rear back but she lost her balance and fell right into the tank. In her surprise, she had sucked in some water. I rushed or rather hobbled up to help her, the water was only about knee deep, but she jumped up by herself and was sputtering and coughing. She was completely wet and in spite of trying to remain sober and apologize, I broke out laughing. I absolutely couldn't help it.

"I finally got over and was going to help her out of the tank but she screamed, 'Don't you touch me! Don't you ever touch me! Don't you ever touch me as long as you live!'

"By then she crawled over the edge of the tank and stomped and sloshed up to the house. Not knowing what else to do. I went on home and thought, 'Boy I sure did blow it this time.'

"It was a few days before I had the nerve to go over there to see her. It was early morning before anyone went to the hay field. I was sure her folks saw me coming and kind of kept out of the way. I walked up to the door and knocked gently, then slowly opened the door and threw my hat in. I waited a bit and was about to leave, minus a hat, when Cindy came to the door with my hat. She had a stern look on her face but she handed me my hat and said, 'It's going to be hot, you might need this.' Then she laughed and threw her arms around my neck and said, 'Now were even, no more pranks!'

"We started seeing a lot of each other then and I think both sets of parents thought it was a good deal. We started to get pretty serious and started talking about the future. I had three brothers and three sisters. I was the youngest and all the rest had left home. They had all married and the brothers had gone into other occupations. Phill had a bulk gas and fuel business. George was in the military and John worked for the county. We talked about me taking over the ranch and all kinds of things and I guess the big mistake was that I never sat down with my dad to discuss these things.

"Fall came and Cindy went to Rapid City and took up nurses training. I had got the cast off my leg and was walking on it to get my strength back. I stayed home that winter and helped dad feed cows. Cindy came home most weekends or I would go to Rapid City so we saw each other almost every weekend except when the weather was bad.

"By this time there was no doubt that we were in love. It seemed like I was just waiting for the that special moment to pop the question.

"Then there was an early spring rodeo that I went to and entered up. Damn, it was good to see the boys again and feel the old camaraderie. My leg felt good and I drew good and won third in the bronc riding. It felt like walking on air to step up to the pay window after the long drought.

"Well there was another rodeo up in North Dakota the next weekend and a bunch of the boys went up to that and I went along. I was hooked again. I called Cindy pretty often and talked with her and got to swing by and see her once in a while. The summer wore on. As July and August came along, I was rodeoing harder than ever. County fair time had come and there were rodeos everywhere. The calls got farther apart and I didn't get to see her very often but I told her I would be back in the fall. I wasn't winning big but I was making it. Fall found me farther south still hitting it.

"It sure wasn't because I had forgot about her. It seemed like I was thinking about her all the time. I had told the boys all about her, they had run out of jokes in return. And I wondered if she knew how much I loved her. It's strange, but before I fell in love, I almost felt like a monk because there just didn't seem to be much in the line of opportunities, but after I met Cindy, it seemed liked temptation popped up at every rodeo. Seemed like there was always an extra girl when the boys met a bunch, or there was a stray here or there. And I <u>was</u> tempted but I wanted to save myself for Cindy. I wished she knew how much I cared but I didn't tell her about the temptations.

"Then there was a big rodeo in Utah that Cindy knew I was entered up in. I was going to call her from there and planned on coming home and asking her to marry me. When I checked in at the rodeo office, the rodeo sec. said that there was a registered letter for me. She said, 'I knew you would be along so I signed for you.' I guessed it was a surprise but was certainly not prepared for the one that it was.

"It was from Cindy and it was a 'Dear John' letter. She told me how hard it was for her to write this letter. She said she would rather have told me personally or at least on the phone but didn't really know how to get a hold of me. Anyway, she said she had come to realize that I was not going to give up rodeoing and she didn't think that was the life for her. She liked rodeos but didn't want them to 'consume' her. She had been 'seeing' Henry Pressly and they were planning on getting married.

"HENRY PRESSLY. Why, he was the town cop. How could she get involved with a small-town cop? I guess I wouldn't have felt so bad if she had ended up with a rancher because I knew she loved animals and the ranching way of life, but a town cop? I just couldn't believe it. I felt shaky.

"I had to sit down to calm my nerves. Then I got mad. How could she do this to me? I felt like busting something or going out and getting drunk. Although I was not a heavy drinker, I had my share with the boys as we went down the road and having fun at an occasional party. But I never did go out to get drunk for the sake of getting drunk. That was about the closest I ever came and in the end I didn't. Damn, I'd show her. I'd go out and win the 'world' and make her sorry that she didn't marry me, and that night I did go out and make the winning ride. I was twenty-one points by one judge and he said, after the performance, that he had never seen me spur like that before. I was taking it out on the horse. But in the end, I was hurt more than anything. And after I had thought about it, I guess I couldn't blame her. How did that song go?

'He loved that damned old rodeo as much as he loved me, someday soon...'

"Even then I think, if I had run back home and talked to her, she would have left that cop and come back to me. I probably would have promised to contain my rodeoing to the local rodeos and thought seriously about the future but that monster PRIDE kept me from it. I didn't go home at all that fall, not even for Christmas. I went south for the winter rodeos, the starvation circuit, but I managed to get by. However, it was long, long time before the hurting was finally over."

By this time the sun had set and the warm colors had changed to the cool colors. The temperature was cooling off too. We sat in silence for a while just looking at the fading light. I was a little surprised at myself, as I had never told anyone about my lost love affair. I thought maybe she would say something about her past life, and perhaps she would have if I had asked but I remained silent.

They were emotional moments and what with it getting cooler, I almost expected her to move closer to me but we sat there staring off into the last light of day, like statues. I turned and looked at her and at that moment, she was again beautiful. She sensed my turning and turned toward me, took my hand and said simply, "I am sorry." Then she got up and said, "Well I guess we better get our rest."

That night, I put her up in the sleeper again, while I made a bed in one of the barns. I laid awake a long time trying to analyze my thoughts. Why didn't I move in on her? Although there was an attraction to her, it seemed there was also a paternal instinct coming to the surface and I felt very protective of her. Then, she was a friend and it certainly felt good to have someone around to talk to besides Rick and Tom. But maybe it was a fact of being subjective. What if I came on strong and she laughed at me? After all, I was probably old enough to be her dad. I couldn't quite figure it out.

I finally fell asleep. That night, I dreamed I was walking down a country road. Up ahead I saw a woman. I hurried to catch up to her and when I got up close enough to see who it was, she turned and it was Sandy. She screamed and ran out of sight. I woke suddenly. I never did get back to sleep. I had never put much stock in dreams or their interpretations but I lay awake until morning trying to figure out what it meant. Since I couldn't sleep anyway, I got up early and checked the stock, made sure they had water and fed them. I was just pulling out of the arena with 'Big Red' when Sandy walked up to the arena and gated me out.

"Why didn't you wake me up to give you a hand?"

"Oh, I couldn't sleep so I thought I might as well feed. Thought as tired as you were, I'd let you catch up on your rest."

We went uptown to eat. The next two days were pretty easy. It wasn't always that way. Sometimes we had long drives between rodeos and lots to do. At times Doc had 'hauls' lined up for the 'pots' and Rick and Tom had driving to do between rodeos but for this Wednesday and Thursday, it was almost like a small vacation.

Having time to kill can also be hard, but in retrospect I look back and think these were two of the happiest days of my life. Tom and Rick kept the motel room and we all borrowed it to clean up in. We double checked the arena and had everything ready to go. Sometimes news people would come out and do pre-rodeo publicity stuff. Interviews and that kind of thing. Of course they would like to talk to a champion but they were never around this early so I would occasionally end up with my pictures in the paper as former bronc rider Buck Compton who is arena director or whatever. I always tried to do my best to help the rodeo along. I was even on radio talk shows and on a few occasions on T.V. talk shows. For the people reading, hearing, and seeing me, they no doubt thought it looked pretty glamorous but they didn't know Buck Compton slept in the sleeper of a gooseneck trailer.

CHAPTER 4

Since we had time to kill, Sandy suggested that we make up a picnic lunch and drive out into the country and see some scenery instead of sidewalks for a change, "If Doc don't mind us using 'Big Red'?"

We filled up the tank and drove out of town on a back road and just went meandering. I found a dirt road that went up a dry wash and small canyon just to see where it went. 'Big Red' was four-wheel drive and there were tire tracks ahead of us, so I wasn't to worried about getting stuck. We drove for several miles churning up dust behind us.

We finally topped out on a high rise where we could see for several miles in every direction. The road or trail dipped down into a draw and kept going somewhere. I suppose it was a shortcut to another road or camp that you could take when it was dry like now. I pulled over and stopped on the top of the rise. We got out and looked the country over in all directions. One could see mostly rolling hills and occasional cut banks and gullies. There were dark lines that were brush covered coulees and canyons. Way off in the distance, we could see a dark line that was the timber along the river and we could just see Roundsville on the river. It wasn't beautiful scenery, as scenery goes, like in the mountains, but it was rather inspiring and the longer one looked, the more it seemed to grow on you. I had been in places like this more than a few times but for Sandy it must have been a first for she gazed in every direction and seemed to drink it in. It was rather breezy up there and we eventually took the lunch and went down the hill a small distance to a sheltered spot with a small clump of trees. We spread the blanket in the shade and Sandy spread out the lunch. She had picked out the makings at a grocery store and put a very good lunch together in short order. I just sat back and watched her. She was revealing new talents all the time. It just felt good to be with her. I wondered if she felt that way about me? I was going to tell her about the dream but then decided not to.

After lunch, we just sat back and relaxed. With the knob of the hill behind us, we could still look out over the surrounding countryside and Sandy seemed absorbed in it.

"This is so...so..., there just aren't words for it, ...mind expanding. You were from a ranching family. You mentioned last night that you had thought about taking over the family ranch. How come you didn't?"

The words hit me like a blow in the stomach and she must have noticed the look on my face.

"Did I say something wrong?"

"No." I said slowly. "It just brings back memories. Yes, I wanted the ranch, but I was hooked on rodeos. Still, I was getting better all the time and I'd get to dreaming that I'd make a bunch and go back and just buy the ranch from Dad. Then there would be no fuss and fights with the brothers and sisters over his or her share. Not that any of us really had anything owed to us.

"Dad had got a hold of a small place after he and mom married and I don't guess any of us really understood how hard Dad and Mom had worked to raise us and keep food on the table. Over the years, he managed to survive and even add some land from time to time. I never knew 'til after he was gone how many times he came close to losing it. I knew things were tough but didn't comprehend it. We always had enough to eat and as a kid, that's about as far as one thinks.

"Anyway, I was rodeoing and winning more all the time. Then I hit three big wins down in Texas. I had money in my pocket like never before. Several of us were sitting in a cafe one morning between rodeos and I picked up the local paper. As I was running through it, I came across an auction ad. I don't know why, but I read it and apparently it was a bankruptcy sale from some oil man who went 'belly up'. I wasn't interested in any oil field equipment but it also had his personal stuff which included a Cadillac.

"Well, we got to joking about it and more as a joke than anything, we went to the auction. I had been traveling with a couple of cowboys who had a van. We were getting by but a half dozen cowboys with all their gear in a van is not exactly traveling in luxury. Anyway, the stuff was going cheap and almost like in a dream, I started bidding on that Cadillac.

"I never really expected to end up with it and was going to quit when the bidding got serious, and all at once the auctioneer yelled, 'Sold to the cowboy in the red shirt.' Well there I was, the owner of a cream-colored Cadillac.

"We went up then and really looked it over now to see what kind of deal I got. Turned out it was a real bargain. Apparently the man had bought it more as a status symbol than anything and had rarely drove it himself. His wife drove it mostly and then not much, as it was a low-mileage rig. All that was about to change.

"Well, I didn't have any shortage of cowboys to travel with now and the passengers put the fuel in the tank and I was sitting on top of the world. The only improvement I put on that old Caddy was a big set of longhorns that I acquired and bolted on the hood. When Buck Compton pulled onto the rodeo grounds, people took notice. I could start to imagine what Casey Tibbs felt like when he would pull in with his maroon Lincoln Continental. Like Casey, wearing maroon shirts to match his car, I got to wearing cream-colored shirts to match mine. And just to commemorate Casey, who I kind of idolized, I wore a maroon silk scarf.

"When I went home for Christmas that year, the family members "oohed" and "aahed" over the car. The only one I didn't impress a damn bit was Dad. He looked it over and walked away and never said a word. Dad had lived through too many lean times and to him, the Caddy was an extravagant toy one could do without. Never mind that I had got it as a bargain. Dad had never owned a new car. He had bought a few new pick-ups in his lifetime but only then because he figured it out to be the best deal for the money. And there were never any frills like chrome or fancy paint jobs on them. In fact this may have been the point of no return for Dad. He may have realized that I was into rodeos for good.

"Anyway, I went back to hitting it hard again and it was the next fall at a rodeo in Nevada when I went to the rodeo office to sign in, when the secretary said there was a message for me to call home. These kinds of messages always made me nervous. You always wonder what's up? Did someone get hurt, or worse yet, killed? Kind of like getting a phone call in the middle of the night. It was never really anything very serious but you always wondered.

"I found a phone right away and called home. Mom answered. 'Oh Will, I am so glad I got a hold of you. I left a message at every rodeo office I could think of that you might be entering.' To mom I was always Will or Willie. She never called me Buck like everyone else.

'What's up mom?'

'Are you coming home for the auction?'

'Auction? Why would I come home for an auction? I could always go to an auction.'

'Oh, I guess I forgot to mention, Dad sold the ranch. It was kind of a rush deal and the party wants possession by the first of December so they can get settled in for the winter. About the only way Dad could get cleaned out by then was to have an auction.'

" 'Dad sold the ranch?' I didn't hear much she said after that. The words kept ringing in my ears. Dad sold the ranch. I went kind of numb and tingly. This has got to be a bad dream. A warning. I will wake up presently and will go home and make arrangements with Dad to take over some way."

'Will, are you still there?'

'Oh, yeah mom.' My mind was racing. 'When did you say the auction was?'

'This coming Thursday.'

'Gosh mom, I don't see how I can. I am entered at the Cow Palace. I'm sitting in eighteenth place and I drew old 'Ham and Eggs' for tonight. I got a real good chance to win it here and if I get lucky in San Francisco, I could go the Finals.'

"I had been dreaming about this for quite a while. I was riding as good or better than I ever had. I was thirty-two. Although I was in relatively good shape for a bronc rider and never suffered anything serious since the broken leg, I had the usual number of bruises and sprains. The aches and pains were getting to me and many were the times when I spent a good part of the night walking the floor instead of sleeping. This might be my best chance. And if I could get to the Finals, there was just a long shot that I could win the world. Of course I realized that it was a long shot. I would practically have to win every go around and all the champs would have to buck off, but dreams are made of stuff like that.

"I tried to explain this to Mom but ended up with, 'I sure would like to make it but I just don't see how I can.'

" 'I understand, Will.' She said in a soft voice and then hung up.

"I began to understand that she understood a lot more than I cared to admit.

"I went back to the Caddy and got my gear bag and saddle out, as it was getting close to show time. Quite a few of the cowboys were around and reading the draw and joshing and joking. When I came in, one of them yelled, 'Here comes old Mr. Lucky. How much did you have to pay the Secretary to draw old 'Ham and Eggs?'

'Well the rest of us will have to ride for second place.'

'If I had that kind of luck I'd go drilling for oil.'

"The joshing went on but I felt kind of tight inside. I should have felt great. I'd drawn Ham and Eggs before and rode him to win a second. He was a good horse. I should have been psyched up but I was not with it at all. When I found out what my horse was, I would usually try to get the ride programmed in my mind if I could. If it was a new horse or one I didn't know anything about, I rode it the best I could, but if I had been on one before or seen it go, I would try to prepare for the ride so that when I nodded for the gate, the sub conscience and reflex actions would take over. You don't have time to stop and think.

CHAPTER 5

"I got my gear out and ready and sat down on my saddle to collect my thoughts. But I wasn't sitting on a bronc saddle. I was sitting on a pony saddle on a little spotted pony on a bluff overlooking a small valley. I was seven years old and already thought I was a cowboy. It was branding time and the cowboys were bringing in the herds. I could see them coming from a ways off as I had a good vantage point. They would bring in the herd and spill them over the edge into this small valley or really a large draw to push them into a set of corrals down at the bottom.

"This wasn't my first branding. Brandings were a neighborhood affair and everyone came to help out. The women brought the whole family and even the babies were brought along and put in the pick-ups or cars. Actually I hadn't missed a one but of course I don't remember the first few. But this was the first one that I was mounted up on.

"Dad had bought me the pony a year before and I spent most of my time with him. Probably would have slept with him if my folks would have let me. His name was Pepper. Not because he was spotted that way but because he was kind of salty when Dad got him. He bucked me off a few times but we finally got to getting along. He just needed lots of riding and he sure enough got that.

"Dad wasn't going to let me bring him but when he saw how crushed I was when he said 'No,' he relented but advised me to keep out of the way. Then he told me to go up on the knob and I could watch the hands bring'em in.

"I was sitting there taking it all in like a king on a throne. Suddenly I saw a few head break off on my side. I don't expect they were going anywhere, just running off to one side a little and there were surely enough cowboys down there to keep everything under control.

I spontaneously kicked old Pepper in the side, bailed off the knob to put them cattle back in the bunch.

"Well, the cattle were used to all the cowboys riding around them but when this kid on a pony exploded out of nowhere into the side of the herd, it not only moved them few on the side, but spooked the whole bunch. That whole herd changed directions in a split second and went right up over the rim and onto the flats. Right about then I realized what I had done and wished a cow would hook my pony and kill me or something. About then Dad rode by hellbent for leather and yelled, 'Damn you, I told you to stay out of the way.'

"It really didn't take the cowboys long to turn them around and bring them back but I felt terrible. I rode off on Pepper and hid. It was Mom that found me, I don't know how, but somehow mothers seem to know stuff like that. She consoled me and talked me into coming back but I didn't ride Pepper the rest of the day. I came back and tried to keep a low profile and hoped no one would notice the tear-stained streaks down my cheeks.

"Old Riley, at least he was old to me, kind of broke the ice. He was an old cowpuncher and my favorite. He looked and acted the part and Riley was never seen in anything but cowboy clothes – dress or work. He always had a word for kids and seemed to like them. They also liked him. He was a bachelor who lived in a shack up on Coon Creek. He worked for various ranchers and was a hand. When he worked for Dad, I followed him around like a puppy.

"At the time, I was too young to understand, but one time when he worked for Dad, someone came by and asked what he was doing. 'Baby-sitting' was his reply as he laughed. He always had a joke and was well liked.

"It was lunch time when I came back to the bunch and I kind of snuck in to get a bite and hoped no one would notice me when Riley said, 'Well, well, how's the stampeder?'

"This of course brought a big laugh and a few more jokes as I lost my appetite and wished the ground would open up and I would disappear.

"About then, I hated him but he came over and slapped me on the back and said, 'You're all right kid. Hell, we all make mistakes.'

'I began to understand then that they were joking and it was just part of my education.

"That evening Dad came over to me and said, 'I didn't mean to be that harsh this morning but if you are ever going to make a hand you're going to have to pay attention and watch the old timers. They're the ones that will teach you.

"I felt a lot better then. And that was one piece of advice that I took. I watched the old timers.

"I was still sitting on my bronc saddle staring into space when a rider came by and kicked my saddle, jolting me back to the present. 'You going to sit there all day or are you going to ride a bucking horse? Your bronc is in the chute.'

"I jumped up and grabbed my saddle and headed for chute number three where Ham and Eggs was standing and waiting patiently for me. He was a big, stout, powerful, strawberry roan horse that weighed about fourteen hundred pounds. He was quiet in the chutes, a smart horse. He didn't waste any of his energy fighting in the chutes, he was saving it all for when the chute gate cracked. I threw the saddle up and eased it down on his back. 'Got to get my mind on this now. He lunges high out of the chutes which makes him hard to mark out but I wasn't worried about that part. Then he would feint to the left and duck right. Or was it feint right and duck left? Damn, I had to get my mind clear. 'Ken, hook my cinch for me will you?'"

'Dad sold the ranch.'

" 'Damn Buck, get that off your mind. Concentrate on this ride. Cow Palace here we come.'

"I measured out the buck rein and eased down into the saddle. Ken asked, 'Are you ready?'

"I tried to shake the cobwebs out of head.

'Ok, you can ride Pepper to the branding but stay out of the way.'

'Well, well, here comes the stampeder.'

'Hell, we all make mistakes.'

'Watch the old timers, they're the ones that will teach you.'

" 'Dad sold the ranch.'

" 'You all right Buck?' Ken's voice came to me.

" 'Yeah, I'm all right. Outside, let's see if this fellow can buck.' As I nodded for the gate.

"Ham and Eggs made his big lunge out of the chute and landed hard on his front feet, then dropped his left shoulder. He sucked back and then ducked to the right and I was eating dirt.

"I lay there for a moment in disbelief and then heard the joshin again, 'Hey, what did you fall off that horse for?'

" ' He didn't fall off, he jumped off.'

" 'He just wanted to get off close to the chutes so he wouldn't have so far to walk back.

" 'Buck is just feeling sorry for the rest of us. Wants to let us win a little.

"Somewhere off in the distance, I could hear the announcer say, 'Hey, here's something you don't see to often, Buck Compton hit the dirt before the whistle. But it's no disgrace to buck off old Ham and Eggs. He is one of the top buckers of the rough string and has been to the National Finals three times.'

"I got up and walked back to the rigging alley. I collected my gear and stowed it in the Caddys trunk. I had needed that win this weekend but if I could win in San Francisco, I might just still make the finals. I crawled into the driver's seat and put my arms on the steering wheel and my head on my arms. I wanted desperately to be alone and collect my thoughts but there were a few of the riders traveling with me to San Francisco, so I had to wait 'til the performance was over.

"Usually when the rodeo was over, the cowboys who were still around would have a beer or two and get into a bull session. The rides would be re-rode and talk of other rides and then to where the next rodeo was. This was if you weren't up someplace else and had to burn rubber to get to the show on time. If I had won some of the loot at this show, I would have been with the bunch and may even have stayed over as we had plenty of time to get to San Francisco. But when the boys finally brought their gear over to the Caddy and saw me behind the wheel, they seemed a little surprised and said, 'Ready to roll?'

" 'I guess.'

"Normally when cowboys have time to kill, they don't kill it on the road. Most drive all the law allows and a little besides. But tonight I drove about 50 M.P.H. and didn't say much the whole way to 'Frisco. It was a painful trip for me and I ended up driving the whole way. I was glad when the bunch fell asleep as I didn't have to manufacture conversation with them.

"We got a room when we got into town and got organized. It was the first time at the Cow Palace for a couple of the boys and they wanted to see where the big event was taking place. So we went on down and looked it over. The rest of the bunch was all excited and the main talk was about the contestants in the thirteenth to eighteenth place as the race would be on to see who would qualify to go to the NFR (National Finals Rodeo).

"I spent a lot of time alone these few days. The other guys were here and there and other cowboys were coming in. There were some parties but I kept to myself pretty much. I was not in a good psychological frame of mind. I knew it and was trying to psyche myself up but wasn't having much luck. 'What the hell,' I tried telling myself. 'What if the ranch is gone? Hell, there's lots of ranches out there. Save up some money and go buy one. The old home ranch wasn't a very good place as ranches go anyway.'

"But somehow I had lost my anchor. I was born and raised on that ranch but now it was like a dry well. I never missed the water 'til the well went dry.

"Eventually, the big day arrived. I checked in and looked over the draw. I had drawn Brown Bomber, not a real good draw but not a bad one either, just average. Well, the odds are against you but sometimes the money is won on an average horse. Sometimes an average cowboy wins. The stock, like the cowboys, have their off and on days. It happens that an average horse on occasion will really turn the crank. Then sometimes a good hand will really try to get wild on a horse like that to make up points for what the horse lacks. Maybe the horse senses this and gives it all he's got. Sometimes he ends up bucking the good hand off.

"When my turn came, I was feeling better and 'screwed' my kak down on Brown Bomber. I nodded for the gate and drove in the steel. I got tapped off right and went on with him 'til I heard the buzzer and the pick-up men moved in and set me on the ground.

" 'How about that folks? Buck Compton, Bad River, South Dakota, makin it look easy.'

"As I walked back I heard, 'A score of sixty-seven for Buck Compton.

"Not bad, but not good enough to make anything at this rodeo. I didn't do any better in the second go so I didn't make my appearance at the pay window when the rodeo was over.

"I was kind of at loose ends. The National Finals were in Los Angeles this year and it was only a short jaunt down there but it was too early to go there. There were some small rodeos in Arizona so several of us went that way to take in a few before the finals. A lot of contestants go to the finals who are not entered there. Those in the sixteenth or seventeenth place just on the chance that someone can't make it and they can move up to fill the gap. But mostly it's just to see the big shots and mix with the 'toughs'. The younger ones dream of the day they will be in there and the 'old has-beens' come down to visit with other has-beens. It is no doubt the number one rodeo in the country where cowboys buy a ticket to attend.

"I wasn't doing any good at any of the rodeos. I was in a slump. Now every cowboy that has gone down the road has gone into a slump some time or other. Some just ride it out, as sooner or later their luck would change. I tried a number of things but nothing seemed to work. It seemed that after Dad sold the ranch, I had not only lost my anchor but also my rudder.

CHAPTER 6

※

"Three of us were heading to Los Angeles. We were in no hurry and just ambling along. Actually, I didn't have my heart in it. We had competed in a small rodeo and I hadn't won anything again. We were going through a small town, just a wide spot in the road when Jake saw a CAFE sign and said 'Let's coffee up.'

"As we got out and looked both ways, someone said, 'We won't have to spend a lot of time deciding which place.' Obviously it was the only cafe.

"Across the street by the only gas station was parked a pick-up with a horse trailer behind. One horse stood in the trailer with his saddle on. A few bumper stickers on the trailer told us this cowboy rodeoed some and was probably a roper.

"The sky was turning overcast and a chill wind whipped up the dust on the street. The horse didn't seem to mind but I ducked my head into the wind and went into the cafe, glad to feel its warmth. As we walked in, the place was almost empty. There were a few sets of tables and chairs and a lunch counter. A lone cowboy sat at the counter. As we entered, he turned, looked us over briefly and nodded. He was slowly turning back to talk to the waitress when he turned and looked again.

"Looking at Jake he said, 'You Jake Spandle?' Jake squinted a few times and jumped up.

" 'Randy Turner?' he yelled and ran over and shook hands.

" 'Well, it's been a long time. Where the hell you been hidin' out? Boys, this is Randy Turner, used to be one hell of a bareback rider. then he disappeared. Hell, I thought maybe you was in jail. What happened?'

" 'Oh, it wasn't that drastic. But almost. I got myself married and thought I better settle down. I still get to a few rodeos but I quit riding the buckers. Don't pay no attention to Jake. I wasn't that good. I do a little roping now.'

" 'Roping?' Jake's voice boomed out. Next you'll be herding sheep.'

"Jake was the oldest of the bunch, as I don't think any of the rest of us had ever met Randy. The joking went on a bit when Randy asked where we were going. 'To the Finals, my boy, to the Finals. Got to win some of the big stuff.' As he winked to the crowd.

"Randy got up and said, 'I've got some chores to do so I've got to be going. Say, if you guys aren't in a hurry, why don't you come out to my place and spend the night. Like for you to meet the wife and kids. There's a small bunkhouse there and you look like you could use some home cooking. I'll call the missus and tell her you're coming.'

"Well, Randy was doing us a favor putting us up for the night and feeding us but I knew we were probably doing him one, too. If you have rodeoed and settle down someplace and happen to be on a 'fly way' you can just about end up running a free motel to cowboys until you go broke, get damned antisocial or end up with a woman who greets all comers with her hands on her hips and a glare in her eye. But if you end up well off the beaten trail, you get lonesome for someone to talk rodeo to. Not that there weren't other guys around to talk to but it would be nice to talk to someone you hadn't seen for a while and catch up on all the old gossip.

"We really didn't have any reason to travel the road we did, we just had time and decided to take a back road and see some new country. Running into Randy had just been a bonus.

"We followed Randy out of town on a dirt road for over ten miles and then suddenly dropped over a ridge into a little valley. About a quarter of a mile down by a small stream was a set of corrals, a small barn, some outbuildings and a large but modest looking house. Dust billowed up as we came into the yard.

"Randy jumped out and said, 'You guys can sleep in the bunkhouse. There's a little stove in there that you can fire up. I may have to hustle up a few blankets.'

" 'Don't bother,' I said. 'We have sleeping bags and bedrolls.

"We stowed our gear and got a fire going in the barrel stove. The bunkhouse was an old railroad refrigerator car. Randy later said that it was pulled into the ranch from Chamber City, thirty-five miles away by a Caterpillar tractor. They wore out three sets of skids getting it there.

"It was getting dark. I stepped out of the bunkhouse and headed for the barn where I saw a light shining through the window. Inside, Randy was milking a Jersey cow. At the end of the small barn was a stall with a calf in it and a young boy was forkin some hay into the manger.

" 'Hi, Mister,' He called. 'You goin to live with us?'

"I walked over and laughed as I replied, 'No I don't think so. Just for tonight.' He was a little fellow with black hair and eyes that shined even in the dim light of the barn. He was about seven years old and he wasn't a bit bashful like some kids are that live out in the country.

" 'This is my pony Peanuts.' He said as we moved to the next stall. He got caught up in a fence and cut pretty bad but Dad says he is going to be okay.'

"Peanuts was a little Appy pony who had apparently cut his hoof and ankle in a barb wire fence. It was pretty well healed up but I could see he was never going to be right again.

"Randy finished milking the cow and turned her out. He poured some milk in a dish for two cats that came from out of nowhere, knowing that when the cow was turned out, it was lunch time. Then Randy introduced his son, Rob.

" 'And Rob this is, what was the name again?'

" 'Buck, Buck Compton.'

" 'Oh yeah, the bronc rider. I shouldn't have forgot that. I guess I was in such a hurry back there in town, it never registered. I remember seeing your name in the rodeo papers. Well it's an honor having you as my guest. Rob run ahead and tell your mother we'll be right in.'

"After Rob had left, he leaned on the rail by the pony, Peanuts. 'I suppose he will die on the place. I cut him out of a fence last spring. He was in pretty bad shape and if I had had a gun with me, I would have put him out of his misery then and there but I didn't, and he hobbled away bleeding. I went back the next day but couldn't find him and figured he had crawled away into the brush someplace and bled to death. Later on, I was helping a neighbor round up his horses and there he was with the bunch. He was crippled up but getting along pretty well. We got him home and he held up all right but as you can see, his hoof is bad and he limps. I should just 'can' him but the kids are so attached to him I don't dare let him go. They still ride him and he is a real baby sitter.'

"We went up to the house and went in. The sweet aroma of supper on a wood cook stove caught my nostrils. The kitchen, dining room, and living room were all in one big room with the range and kitchen appliances on the far end. A dark-haired woman was next to the stove with her back to us as we entered. She turned around as Randy set the milk pail on the table. She was dark skinned, apparently Mexican, and wasn't at all hard to look at. Randy introduced her as Bonita and when she later set a big bowl of chili on the table for supper, there wasn't much doubt about her ancestry.

"Randy strained the milk into glass jugs and took them out to the spring house to cool. He brought back a cool one for supper. He beat on a triangle hanging by the door and Jake and Broomby came in from the bunk house. He introduced around again introducing his second son, Richie, who was four years old.

"As we all sat down to the big table, Randy asked the blessing and we dug into that big bowl of chili, fresh biscuits, honey, butter, milk or coffee. It was a real homey atmosphere way out away from everywhere, it seemed, and the only foreign noise was the faint hum of an engine off in the distance by the machine shed that ran the generator to give him electricity for his lights and a few other things on the ranch.

"It was almost silent for a while as Jake and Broomby dug into that chili like they hadn't eaten in days. The boys dug in too, but I got a little knot in my stomach. Here was a man who had quit rodeos and was apparently owner of a ranch. For a minute, I hated him.

"After supper was over, we leaned back, Jake and Randy mostly got to talking about the rides they had made and others had made or not made, and I could see, though Randy had quit the circuit, his heart was still back there.

"Finally Jake popped out, 'How the hell did you get this ranch any way? Rob a bank or did Bonita own it and you copped on to her?' Jake never did have much tact and sometimes it was down right embarrassing to be around him.

"Randy just laughed and said, 'Lucky. Just lucky. In the first place, it's a long way from being paid for but we have a home at the time. I never had a ranch background. My dad was a mechanic but I had wanted to be a cowboy from as far back as I can remember. When I got into high school, I started rodeoing. Some at high school rodeos and hitting a few small ones but of course not making anything. Then I went to work on a ranch and believe me, that was a lot rougher on me than rodeo was. Those cowboys 'jobbed' me more than a few times but I wanted to be a hand so bad that I toughed it out.

" 'Then I started to get the hang of bronc riding and started making a few bucks at that. But mostly I dreamed of having a ranch of my own and so I worked on ranches all over to learn the trade. Ten years ago I met Bonita at a rodeo in Eagle Run and hell, boys, I fell in love.' At this Bonita turned and her face lit up with a big smile.

" 'I tried saving money for a while and eventually we got married. We got a job looking after some cattle in the mountains and that's where we spent our honeymoon, in a tin shack looking after those cows. It was great but I knew we were never going to get a ranch that way. That fall I got a job working construction. Didn't care all that much for it but it paid a whole lot more. Bonita worked as a waitress and we managed to save a little nest egg. Then Robby came along and kind of took care of the nest egg.'

"Rob was sitting beside his dad and at that, Randy ran his hand through his hair and you could see that whatever Rob cost, he was worth a million times more.

" 'We went back to working ranches and about resigned to be a working cowboy all my life when I drove into Chamber City a few years back and heard about old Chub Hartman. Chub was a bachelor and owned this place. Run it by himself and was one tough cowboy. Chub had got into a wreck with his horse when he roped a cow on frozen icy ground. The cow had hit the end of the rope and busted herself but when she got up, she came after the horse. Chub was dally-roping and threw the rope away but on the slippery ground the horse couldn't maneuver fast enough and that old cow caught his old pony plumb in the midsection and piled them all up. When they got untangled the cow ran off and the horse ran home leaving Chub over a mile from the buildings with a broken leg and nobody in the world who knew where he was or what shape he was in.

" 'Well, like I said, Chub was tough. He got into a sitting position and put the broken leg on top of the good leg. Then he slid himself by his hands and arms on the seat of his pants, backwards 'til he got home. Took him over ten hours. Passed out a few times but he made it.

" 'Then he hauled himself up and into his pick-up truck and drove to Circle where I met you fellows this afternoon. It was past midnight and everything was closed. He pulled up behind Lyle's Service Station where Lyle lived with his family, and laid on the horn. When I think back on it, it's funny that horn was still working because that pick-up was in pretty tough shape and Chub only fixed whatever was an absolute necessity to keep it going. Anyway, he got Lyle out and told him he needed a ride to Chamber City to the Doc. "And send somebody out to look after my horse."

" ' Lyle transferred him into his station wagon where he promptly passed out again.

" 'Lyle got him into town and into the hospital, then went back and personally went out to check on the horse. He was waiting patiently at the corral gate. Lyle unbridled and unsaddled him and turned him loose and got back to Circle just in time to open the service station. Cowboy's weren't the only ones to put in long days.

" 'Chub was pretty battered and bruised besides the fractured leg and the doc kept him in the hospital a couple of days. Chub wanted to go back to the ranch as soon as the leg had a cast on it but that was out, and the doc wouldn't let him go. He was a cantankerous old cuss and finally raised enough commotion to where the doc turned him loose but not to go back to the ranch. He checked into the Cattlemen Hotel uptown and pestered anyone who would listen for a ride back to the ranch. But the doc had spread the word and everyone had excuses why they couldn't do it just then "but in a few days."

" 'About that time I came into town looking for work. I met old Chub in the lobby of the Cattleman, feeling sorry for himself, and hit him up for a job as he needed someone to look after the place. He only ran about 125 cows and hadn't hired anyone for years. He used to hire hands at haying time when he put up hay with horses but in the later years he got mechanized. Although he was really rough on machinery, he ran the place all by himself. He traded work with the neighbors when it came to working stock and got by. He said he really didn't need any help, all he needed was to get back to the ranch. He was a tough old coot and I believe he would have made it too but being alone out there with a cast on his leg meant another accident might be his last.

" 'I left him alone for a while and talked around to a few other people in town and then went to see the doc. Several of the towns people including doc, had a little 'committee meeting' concerning Chub and decided that going back to the ranch would be a real morale booster but he couldn't be alone.

" ' I went back to see Chub. My ace in the hole was that he desperately wanted out of town. I said, "Look, give me a job looking after the place. We'll take you out to the ranch and Bonita can do the cooking and whatever, and you tell me what to do. The wages will probably be less than what it is costing you to stay in town." That done it and we loaded him up, picked up some supplies and headed for our new home.

" 'It took a few days to get the house cleaned up and settled in. Chub was happy to be back and I started in learning what needed to be done. Calving season was about to begin although Chub ran a kind of rawhide operation and the cows calved out on the range. He did keep the first calf heifers up in a trap pasture and looked after them. He had also done a lot of riding and seemed to know where everything would be at any given time. But Chub was in his sixties and the accident had left him in worse shape than we originally figured, including himself. I think he had figured on there being a temporary situation and when the cast came off, he would be back in the saddle. He had to go back to the Doc once in a while, a trip that Bonita usually made.

" 'He had never married and I think he appreciated having a woman fuss over him some. Anyway, he got looking forward to the trip to town. Bonita, Rob and Chub would stop at a cafe and have lunch. He thrived on Bonita's cooking and put on a little weight. He eventually got rid of the cast and hobbled around the ranch and helped me out. Mostly finding things and giving orders. Got to saddling up once in a while and riding out but I could see he was hurting even though he wouldn't admit to it. He had some bottom land along the creek, that usually flooded in the spring and made enough of a hay crop to feed the cattle thru the lean part of winter. I put up all the hay.

" 'Came fall we started working the cattle. One day, I ran in the horses and Chub saddled up old Buck, a big buckskin. Buck was feeling good and when Chub stepped up, he kind of blew the cork. He wasn't bucking that hard, just feeling good and Chub stayed with him but I was afraid he might get hurt again so rode up and pulled up on Buck. Chubs' face was a pasty gray and white.

" ' "You all right?"

" ' "Yeah, I can ride the S.O.B." And he did but I could see he was uneasy all day as we gathered the stock.

" 'That night when we unsaddled, he was sore and stiff. He turned slowly and looked at me and said, "I'm guess I am going to have to admit, I just ain't the hand I used to be."

" 'This must have been a hell of a blow to his pride as I'm sure he was one hell of a cowboy in his day.

" ' "Chub" I said in all sincerity, "If I get to be half the hand you are, I will consider my self arrived."

" 'I didn't know what kind of shape Chub was in financially but expected he had some cash put aside somewhere as the bills got paid but I wasn't collecting much in the line of wages. About this time Bonita was expecting our number two son. Winter was coming on and we needed a house so we just kind of let things slide which I realize now was not good business management but in my case it worked out. Remember I said LUCK.

" 'We had rounded up and sold the calves except for some replacement heifers. Culled out some cows and settled in for winter. I fed when they needed feeding and kept fixing and puttering around the place.

" 'One winter day, a wet heavy snow had come down and there wasn't much to do. I had brought a saddle in and was fixing on that. I had been putting it off but knew I had to bring it up sooner or later and thought this was a good time. Chub had been giving me some help on the saddle and seemed to be in a good mood.

" ' "Chub, I think there's something we better get straightened out. We never have settled up on my wages. My car needs repairing and Bonita is expecting right about calving time. I think we better get squared up and then if you think you can get along without me, I'll go look for another job."

" 'Chub was silent for a long time. I got to thinking he hadn't heard me or tuned me out. I was about to repeat myself when he turned slowly towards me. I could see the hint of a tear in his eye.

" ' "Randy, I never had much of a family life. My dad was a rough old cowpuncher and was gone most of the time and mom had it pretty tough. I had an older brother who was killed in World War II. I started cowboying pretty damned young and thought I was tough as hell. And I guess I was. Like a lot of cowboys, I wanted a ranch of my own. I saved what money I could but even then it was tough to get started. Finally happened onto this place. Used to be a pretty big operation, that's why the big house. But the owner used a lot of leased range, didn't have all that much deeded land. When he lost that, things went down hill. Finally lost it and the banker was sitting on it. It didn't have enough acreage to attract a big rancher and what with the buildings, it made the land too expensive for some one to buy looking for additional pasture. It sat empty for a couple of years and on occasion I would ride through it and look it over.

" ' "Finally one day when I was feeling brash, I rode in to see the banker. I must have hit the right day because when I came out of that bank, I was no longer a cowboy, but a rancher. Right then and there it changed my whole life. I wanted to go down to the first saloon and celebrate a little but realized I couldn't afford to. I went on home and started the serious business of putting the ranch on a paying operation. I guess I would like to have found someone to share this with but I wanted to get the ranch on a paying proposition before I looked for a mate. The years slipped by and eventually, I got in a rut and now here I am.

" ' "You folks came along and cleaned up the house. Afraid you're the only family life I ever really knew. I feel like Robby is my grandson. That accident left me in worse shape than I care to admit and I know I can't run this place alone anymore. Why don't you stay on 'til spring and this will let your accumulated wages serve as a down payment on the place? We'll go see the banker and work out a plan where you can buy it."

" 'Hell, I thought I was tough but suddenly I had a little trouble seeing the saddle I was working on. Something about moisture in my eyes. I got up and excused myself. Said I had to go look after the horses. I went out to the barn and couldn't believe what I had heard. I wanted to whoop and holler but I didn't want old Chub to see a grown man cry. Bonita had been sewing and I didn't think she had been listening but the next thing I knew, she was standing beside me crying, too.

" 'We made out a deal to make payments on the ranch once a year at shipping time. Old Chub stayed with us and helped out a bunch but he kept getting worse and finally had to stay in town. We would pick him up and bring him out to the ranch occasionally, like branding time, Thanksgiving and Christmas.

" 'He finally ended up in a nursing home. Tough way for an old cowboy to go. Then one day we got the news we were expecting. We had the burial here at the ranch. Figured that's where he would want to be. He never left a will and apparently didn't have any relatives, but the county had his accounts from his later bills and nursing home so I am still making payments.

" 'I don't guess the ranch can ever pay for itself although, with good range management and improvements, it might be built up to carry 200 head. So I went to working out. Do a lot of day cowboy work and anything else I can find. Bonita even went to waitress work once in a while up at the cafe where I met you guys.

"We then got to talking about us fellows going to the Finals and Randy mentioned how he would like to go just once but it didn't look like he'd ever make it. I carefully asked him why and he replied that he needed someone to look after the place mostly, and although we talked of other things it kind of kept coming back to that. And then he mentioned, kind of low that if he don't make it this year it will no doubt be along time as Bonita is expecting again and next year there will be a baby. And then I came up with one of those impulses of mine that seem to get me into trouble.

" 'Look, why don't you and Bonita go this year? I'll stay here and look after the kids and the place. I didn't really have my heart set on going anyway since I didn't qualify. I guess I was just kind of following the herd. It'll do you good to get away a few days and get a vacation."

"Randy sure perked up after that and he and Bonita talked some and said he would let us know in the morning. We all turned in and I suppose they talked half the night.

CHAPTER 7

※

I hadn't been looking at Sandy as I was talking. The undulating hills and soft colors blended into a haze on the horizon and it seemed I could see the past unfolding before me in that vast panorama. I stopped talking a moment and slowly turned to look at her. Her back was resting against a leaning tree and her head was bent forward with her chin on her breast. I thought she had fallen asleep from my dull narrative but when I stopped talking she slowly raised her head and turned toward me. She didn't speak, but her eyes said 'Yes? Please go on.'

"Randy banged on the triangle again in the morning and we rounded out and came over for breakfast. He was all smiles.

" 'Well, we counted the change in the sugar bowl and decided we can go. I'll show Buck around here as to the chores. We'll take Richie with us, and Robby, you get to be foreman and keep Buck company.'

"I guess they felt that Robby shouldn't miss any school. I personally thought that he would learn more in a couple days at the Finals than a whole week of school but I kept my opinion to myself. I'm sure Robby felt the same way but he put up a brave front.

"Randy showed me around the chores that needed doing. There really wasn't that much, more of a baby-sitting job than anything. One of the chores was graining the horses each morning. Ranchers don't all do things the same way, it's whatever works out best for you. Some ranchers keep up a wrangle horse to run the others in with in the morning if you need to. Some just keep them up in a trap pasture or whatever. Randy had a pasture that he let them run in but he grained them every morning in the corral. That way they were always there each morning whether he needed them or not. He only had four horses at the time.

"As he opened the gate to let them into the feed bunk, a big Chestnut horse was first. He was very aggressive but a beautiful horse. He would fight for the best spot and Randy had to put the grain in several places so they would all get a chance to eat. I commented on the chestnut and he said he hadn't got around to riding him yet. He had bought him that spring for a bargain but every time he needed to ride, he needed a horse he could plum depend on and so had passed him by. He would get around to riding him this winter when he had time.

"They spent the rest of the day getting ready to go. Bonita baked and packed a big box of lunch and things to eat. It was clear that they were counting pennies and going as cheap as they could. The next morning they were up early, packed the station wagon, piled in and waved good-bye. With Jake and Broomby, it was not going to be a dull trip.

"Later, the school bus came by and picked up Robby. I waved him off and said I'd see him when he got home. The bus came into the homestead in good weather but if the roads got bad, Randy drove him to high ground in the pick-up.

"Well, I went out to do my chores. I went to the corral and sure enough the horses were there. I poured the feed and let them in. I couldn't help but admire that chestnut horse. He was about as pretty a put-together horse I ever saw. Then I thought over what Randy had said. He was a 'bargain.' That meant there was something wrong with him 'cause horses that look like that just aren't bargains. And then I thought about Randy putting off riding him. Randy had been a bronc rider but he was married now with a family and probably a lot more cautious than he used to be. With most fellows it don't seem to make much difference but I had seen more than a few tough hands that quit the rough string when they got 'responsibilities.' I suspected Randy had run onto the horse and thought it was too good a deal to pass and now was getting cold feet. Maybe I was selling Randy short but I was intrigued. The more I thought about it, the more I wanted to find out. He DID say I could ride any of the horses I needed to. Suddenly I felt a great need. I was a little apprehensive as a man don't usually mess around with another man's horse without permission. Some men are fussier with their horses than they are with their women.

"Well, what the hell, Randy wasn't here. I looked the layout over and next to the corral where the horses were feeding was a big round breaking corral complete with a snubbing post in the center. I looked it over and it was in kind of bad shape but looked like it could be fixed up. Probably hadn't been used much since Chub ran the place.

"I spent the rest of the morning scrounging up material to fix up the pen to where I thought it would hold. Actually, it was more of a bluff fence than anything. It would hold if he didn't call my bluff.

"I went in at noon, made myself a lunch and thought about the strategy I would use on the horse. I went out to the corral and opened the gate to the round pen. The chestnut was very aggressive and sorting him out was easy as he was the first horse through the gate. Probably thought he was getting out. I was about to turn the other horses out when I decided to keep them up just in case old 'Bargain' broke out with some equipment on him.

"I went into the barn to see what was around for gear. There were a couple of ketch ropes hanging on the wall, a good stout halter that would do and some other ropes. I looked over a couple of saddles and then decided to use my old 'committee.' I had to do a little adjusting to the stirrup fenders and things like that. I wasn't planning on making a high point ride, I just wanted to see if this horse could be made to amount to anything.

"I carried my gear into the pen and up to the snubbing post. Then I shook out a big loop in my ketch rope. Now I am a rider, not a roper but most any ranch cowboy has done some roping; but that wasn't my long suit. When I shook out a loop, Bargain started running around the pen and I let fly. If he had had horns, I would have caught him but the edge of the loop settled on his nose and he was going too fast to 'fish' it on him so I lost the first try.

"The second time, I led him a little more and settled the loop around his neck. I expected a jerk and I was ready for him as I dug in my heels and he started to drag me but it surprised him and it broke his stride. I quickly jumped to the snubbing post and threw a half hitch over it. As he ducked and started to run again, he hit the end of the rope but this time there was no give and he spun around and faced me. I guess I'm not a professional horse breaker but I had broke out more than a few colts in my younger days. A colt will usually choke down the first time he's roped and you have a short time to put on a breaking halter. Then you go to halter breaking him one way or another. You then go on to finish breaking him. Again, there are many different ways and most horse breakers end up with their own ideas and systems. I would much rather work with colts that nobody had messed with than with a horse that had learned lots of bad tricks. But this time I didn't have that choice.

"I kind of figured that Bargain was already halter broke and I was right. I started talking to him and taking up slack and he cautiously walked up to the snubbing post but he was snorting and blowing and watching me all the while. When he got up to the snubbing post, I started petting him and rubbing him on the neck and around the head and then slowly slipped the halter on him. He seemed to settle down some and I got the saddle blanket and slipped that around him. He had been through this before so I popped it a few times but he didn't explode. Next I threw the saddle on and he stood for that.

"This is getting too easy. I am sure he has got some bad habits someplace.

"I kept wondering what they were. I reached under for the cinch with a cinch hook I had made. I wasn't going to take too many chances 'til I got to know him a little better. I ran the latigo through the cinch ring and gave it a pull.

"Bargain let out a beller and went straight up and over backward. I thought that halter was stout but he snapped it like a piece of string. He jumped up and ran around the pen again. I roped him again, and again he came up to the snubbing post. He had shook the saddle loose. I threw a double half hitch around the post and gathered the gear.

" 'Well, we are learning your little tricks.'

"I knew he would do this again, so I patched up the halter, put it on him but tied it loose with slip knot that would come out when he pulled back. Then I carefully slipped a soft rope around his front ankles and gave a turn around the snubbing post. I went through the saddling process again. As I pulled the cinch, I gave it an extra tug and he bellered and blew again.

"This time I was ready for him. I grabbed the rope that was around his front ankles and he came down on his side. I quickly pulled his feet as high as I could and took a double half hitch around the snubbing post. I took another rope and gathered up those hind feet and trussed them to the front feet. Then I started rubbing him all over and talking to him. He looked at me as much as to say, 'How did I ever get into a mess like this?'

" 'Well, old Bargain, you aren't as smart as you thought you were. Now you might as well quit acting foolish and start acting like a horse. You and me are going to get along just fine.'

"I sat down on him and kept talking to him. I recalled a Will James print of a cowboy sitting on a horse that was laying down all tied up. The cowboy was smoking a cigarette and looking off into the distance. Well, that was one bad habit I didn't take up myself but I could picture myself in a Will James painting, sitting on this horse all the same.

"Now with colts, you have to show them that you aren't going to hurt them and eat him up. A good bit of the breaking process is to show him you're his friend. He has a natural fear of you and when he gets over that, the rest is just training. And a colt will shiver and shake 'til he gets over that. But Bargain was one cool dude. He hadn't even broke a sweat, but I figured he was learning just the same. When I figured he had 'soaked' long enough, I let him up. I left the rope around his front feet and resaddled him. This time he stood there like a gentleman.

"Now it was time to see what he was going to do with a man in the saddle. I didn't think that he was going to be that much of a bucker or he would already be in some stock contractor's bucking string. But I was sure I wasn't done finding out his string of dirty tricks either. I put on a hackamore, I didn't want to use a bit yet 'til I found out if he knew anything. I might have to pull him around some and a bit could tear up his mouth if he wasn't used to it. I carefully tied a rope around his front feet with a slip knot in it and took the long end in my hand. I gathered the rein in my hands, took a handful of mane, sprung into the saddle and pulled the rope loose from his front feet.

"I expected him to blow a cork but he just stood there. The reprieve was all right with me as it gave me time to set my feet in the stirrups. I nudged him with a spur but he still stood there.

" 'Well, we aren't going to get any dancing done this way,' I socked the spurs to him.

"He bogged his head and went to bucking. As I had figured, he wasn't that tough a bucking horse. He bawled and bellered and threw a lot of bluff with it but he was mostly a stiff-legged jumper and after about ten jumps he broke into a run around the pen. I let him run a while to wear him down. After a while he slowed to a trot. He was a little rough but I had been on lots worse. I started in to rein on him and surprisingly he responded but he sure wasn't sharp. Someone had done some breaking on him someplace but had not put a finish on him. I rode him around some more reining him both ways and then rode up to the edge of the pen and said, 'Whoa!'

"He stopped and stood there. I thought maybe that was lesson enough for today. I took a short hold on the near rein and stepped off quickly. He jerked sideways and hit the edge of the pen fence then tried to lunge ahead. I was expecting something like this and jerked hard on the rein and he stopped and stood still. I talked to him some more, telling him he'd only get a sore head doing stuff like that and slowly unsaddled him and turned him loose. He ran around the pen some whinnying.

"I thought he might be a little hard to gather in the morning so I left him in the pen and turned the others out. I carried water for him and gave him some hay. Also a few handfuls of grain to sweeten his disposition.

"When the school bus came in, Robby finished the other chores and milked the cow. Robby was a delight to be around. He was quite a talker and asked a million questions, especially about rodeos. He already had the bug. He noticed Bargain in the pen and asked how come. I knew I couldn't keep it a secret for long, so I told him I had rode him. I asked him what he knew about the horse, (from the mouths of babes comes the truth) but he didn't know any more than I did. I did ask him a favor though. I asked him not to tell his dad, to let me do that. So we shook on it, real man to man.

"The next day, I went at it again. I had to rope him to catch him but he led up to the snubbing post. I used the cinch hook to put the rope around his front feet. He didn't seem to want to fight too much but I wasn't far enough along to test him that much. He remembered the deal from yesterday, and I saddled him with no trouble. This time I took the rope off his front feet and sprung into the saddle and he promptly exploded. He went through his stiff-legged jump and his bawling and bellering and then broke into a run.

"This time I started to rein him around and he came around pretty well. He was learning way too fast for a green colt so I figured someone had him pretty well started once before. After I rode him a while in the pen putting him through his starts and stops and all of that, I rode back to the snubbing post and dismounted. He tried to jerk away again but I had a good hold and held him. I left his halter on under the hack and tied this up short to the snubbing post. I stepped up on him but he stood and I dismounted again. This time he stood. I got on and off several times and he seemed to be resigned to it so I untied him and led him around some. Got on and off several times more.

"Then I tied him up again, took the hack off and put a bridle on with a snaffle bit to see how he would take it. At first he kind of slobbered and rattled it but he settled down real fast. I left him tied like that and went about the few chores, checking on him every little bit. Then I unsaddled him, gave him a little grain and turned him loose.

"After I had my noon lunch, I went back to the breaking pen, roped Bargain and saddled up again. He jumped a little when I cinched up but otherwise behaved pretty well. When I stepped up though, he exploded again going through his stiff-legged bucks. Then he settled down to a run and stopped when I whoaed.

"I rode him around the pen some and got to wondering if that was why he had been sold. I knew a stock contractor once who had a grulla horse he used for a pick-up horse. He was a hell of a good horse but every time you stepped up on him, he would explode, just about like this fellow. Then when he had bucked for about 200 feet, his head came up and he was all business. Got so when it was show time, the pick-up man would step up and they would do their thing right in the arena. Then he would ride back to the entry gate, pick up the American flag and lead the Grand Entry. The crowd always got a big kick out of it.

"Still I wondered if Bargain had any more tricks up his sleeve and figured it was time to find out. I had kept the other horses penned up as I didn't want any loose horses running interference. I opened the gate to the pasture, stepped up and rode out. He wanted to bolt but I held him in for the first couple of hundred yards and then let him out some. We were getting by and I was running him around some. We came up on a rise and there was a small grove of scattered aspen on the side hill. I decided to ride there and see what was on the other side.

"As we got onto the grove, he suddenly bogged his head, took the bit in his teeth and stampeded into the trees. He was riding tight to the trees on one side and then the other, trying to rub me off. I was really going through gymnastics as I jerked one leg up into the saddle and then the other as he was missing those trees by inches. We managed to get through the grove without him dislodging me or my getting hit and probably breaking a leg. After we got through the grove, his head came up and he acted like nothing had happened. He was a cool dude. I rode around some then eventually on home to put him away. I also acted like nothing out of the ordinary had happened.

"The next morning I went out to do chores again after Robby had caught the bus. I knew old Bargain would pull that stunt again so I looked around the barn and found an old discarded broken up harness that had a broken tug. I cut about a three-foot chunk out of that tug and made myself a quirt. I drilled a hole in both ends and put a popper on one end and a leather thong on the other to put around my wrist.

"I saddled up again and he went through his buck again. Since he always had the same pattern, he was not hard to ride and in fact I was getting quite a kick out of it. I'd be talking to him all the time and laughing at him telling him what a fool he was making of himself. When he settled down, I opened the gate and headed out into the pasture. I rode off at an angle to the aspen grove and I'm sure he figured I was going to avoid it but just as we were about to pass it, I reined him directly to it and through it. When we reached the trees, sure enough he bogged his head and stampeded trying to rub me off again. But this time I was ready for him.

"In between the times I was jerking my legs up and saving my life, I went to 'tuning' on him with that leather bat. I like a bat like that, better than a round quirt as it won't cut up or really hurt a horse but the horse sure does think he is getting hurt when that thing slaps down on him.

"He finally decided he was getting the worst of it and pulled up his head and acted like a gentleman. We rode to the far end of the pasture, up and down a few dry washes and then back through the aspen grove. He was about to duck his head once but I got the jump on him and gave him a swat with the bat on the side of his neck and we rode on through without a hitch.

"The next day was about a repeat of day number three. We rode through the aspen again and just before we got to the trees, I started slapping the bat on my chaps. He sure did pay attention and we rode on through without any adventures. That evening after I unsaddled him and gave him his feed, I turned him out. I couldn't keep him up all the time and Randy was going to be home sometime.

"That night I heard a car drive in and sure enough in the morning they were home and Bonita had breakfast on the table. They had had a good time meeting friends and visiting and brought me up to date as to who was winning what. Jake and Broomby had stayed and got in with another bunch so they had come back alone. Robby was very quiet at breakfast. He was almost busting to keep from telling Randy I had been riding Bargain and he didn't dare say anything for fear that he would blurt it out.

"After breakfast, we were nursing that last cup of coffee.

"Randy said, 'I suppose you will be moving on?'

"I smiled, 'Is that an invitation to leave?'

" 'Oh no, it's just that I thought...' and he turned kind of red.

"I laughed. 'I shouldn't have put you on like that but if you don't mind, I would like to stay a few more days and see a little more of the ranch. It's kind of relaxing to be off the circuit a little bit. Maybe it will be good for me in the long run.

"I didn't tell him I was in a slump but I had been doing a lot of thinking and trying to straighten out my thoughts and not having much luck. Randy had rodeoed enough to realize the joking and laughed himself as he said, "You can stay as long as you want or 'til I kick you out.'

"As we saw Robby off to school, I shook his hand and said , 'Thanks trooper.'

"He grinned from ear to ear and replied, 'I am sure glad you are going to stay a few more days Buck. See you,' and he ran for the bus.

"Randy and I went out to do the chores and he opened the gate to let the horses in. Three horses ran in for their feed but Bargain hung back from the gate about 150 feet.

" 'That's strange,' Randy remarked, mostly to himself. 'That chestnut is usually the first one in.'

" 'Why don't you go about your chores, I think he'll come in.'

"I was guessing that if we got out of sight, he would let his desire for food overcome his reluctance to come in, but I was pretty much on edge. We might have to saddle up and run him down. When Randy left I ducked around the corner of the barn so we were both out of sight, Bargain ran back and forth a few times but his weakness for grain overcame him and he slipped into the corral up to the feed bunk. I ran to the gate and slammed it shut just as he spun around to make a break for it. Seeing that he was outwitted, he walked slowly back to the bunk to finish his feed.

"I didn't know what Randy had planned for the day but he came by again, probably to turn out the horses. He just naturally looked them over, and though Bargain had rolled and scratched himself, the sweat lines from the saddle blanket were very obvious.

"Randy stood and looked at him for what seemed a long time. I had been meaning to tell him but didn't know quite how to break the ice. Finally the problem resolved itself as he slowly said, 'I don't recall telling you to ride the Chestnut.'

" 'Well you didn't tell me NOT to ride him.'

"I felt a lot better when I saw him slowly smile and answer, 'Yeah, I guess you're right. How was he?'

"We sat down then and I related the past four days to him. I finished up with, 'I think he'll make a horse but he's going to need a lot of wet saddle blankets and I doubt that he'll ever be a kid's or a woman's horse.'

" 'Well, if he needs riding, let's do some now. I have some cows in the back pasture that we can move up front in case the weather gets bad and I need to cake'em.'

"I had to rope old Bargain again and saddled him as usual. When I stepped aboard, he went through his stiff-legged buck again and we rode off.

"Randy laughed, "Good way to get the blood circulating on a cool morning.' Randy was sure watching the Chestnut. 'Seeing as how you kind of broke him, did you name him?'

" 'I have been calling him Bargain, as Robby said that's what you got him for.'

" 'Well I'm not sure that he is yet, but Bargain it is.'

"We found the cattle and got them moved. It was not a tough gather. Randy kind of kept tabs on his stock and rode his pastures pretty often so his stock didn't get all that wild. A few miles south, on a lower elevation, were some bigger outfits. They usually worked the cattle at least twice a year but a cow could survive all year long on her own and some did. And got pretty wild. In fact that was some of Randy's day cowboy work, helping to catch some of the wild cows.

"Still, we had some rough ground to cover and had to do a little hard riding to get the job done. I was a little apprehensive as to what would happen when we had to produce, but Bargain seemed to thrive on it. He had gas. And he was tough. He really hadn't been conditioned and yet as we rode back to the buildings, he seemed as fresh as when we rode out in the morning.

"It was about three o'clock when we rode in and I anticipated lunch when Randy exclaimed, 'Oh my gosh, I forgot to tell Bonita we were riding off. She would have had dinner ready at noon.' It was quiet as we went into the house. There was a new bowl of chili in the oven and a very quiet Bonita sewing in the rocker. But Randy apologized and told her about the horse and she thawed out as we commenced eating.

"In talking it over we both kind of came to the conclusion that who ever had owned the horse had green broke it and sold it to someone who was not cowboy enough for it and the horse had got the bluff on him. Or perhaps the party had raised it and sent it out to get broke.

CHAPTER 8

"That night the phone rang and Randy answered it. 'Yep. Sure. Six you say? Fifty dollars a head eh? Sure. Get right on it.'

"As he came back to sit down he filled me in. 'Sid Meddows has just finished gathering in the Green Canyon Pasture. He thought they had all of them but someone riding thru said they saw what they thought was six head. Could be more. He'll give me fifty dollars a head delivered to where he can pick them up in a truck or trailer. It's rough country. You want to come along?'

" 'You ain't big enough to beat me into staying home.'

"We were up way before dawn and ate breakfast alone. Bonita had made a lunch the night before.

" 'We won't have time to run down Bargain, so we'll just have to see if he comes in by himself.' Randy let out a yell and the horses came running.

"I was on the gate and when I heard them run in, I slammed it shut. Randy came with a lantern and, lo and behold, there was Bargain with the rest of them. We saddled all four and loaded up in the stock trailer. Bargain had been hauled before and loaded without trouble.

"Randy tied a few hay bales on the side of the trailer and put some grain in the pick-up. We drove about twenty miles to the Green Canyon Pastures. We crossed a cattle guard and went another three miles down a winding canyon road to a small, flat clearing and stopped. Here there was a small shack and dilapidated corral and a spring where stock and wildlife came to drink. We unloaded the horses just as it was getting daylight.

"Randy had been here before but it had been a few years and he went to look over the corral to see if it would hold stock if we caught any. It looked like it needed a little repairing. Although we hadn't planned on using it, we looked in on the shack. As we opened the door, several pack rats scampered off. The place hadn't been used for some time and it looked it but there was a stove there with a bunk and some benches and a table. Also a wood box full of firewood. It had been a line camp at one time, I suppose.

"The pasture was approximately 8,000 acres and that is not all that big but this one was rough. It consisted of a series of canyons and hogbacks made by a number of small streams, when it rained, that drained into a large stream and eventually found its way to the Green River.

"Randy looked over the lay of the land. There was a spring on the hillside behind the corral with a pipe coming out of it. The pipe drained into the big tank and whatever water the stock didn't drink, spilled over into a little draw on its way to Green River. I kind of wondered why they hadn't built a big pen around the spring and tank and then when the cattle came in, they could just close the gate but I didn't voice my ideas.

"Randy looked all around the tank and I was to get some lessons in tracking that day. He showed me where the cattle had been coming in and how to tell if the track was fresh or a day old or older. Actually, I flunked that class. Even after he showed me, I really couldn't tell the difference. I had heard all kinds of stories about trackers and have come to the conclusion that it is a talent or gift, something like music. I have seen some fellows that just early on, picked up a guitar and could pick out almost anything on it and others could try all their lives and never hit two chords right in a row. Anyway, Randy said there were cattle there sure enough but he didn't know just how many. Said he didn't have enough Apache in him.

"We tightened the cinches and I stepped up on old Bargain and he promptly did his thing. If I had been alone, I would have taken him into the old corral first, not that I was worried about riding him but if he was bucking off into the brush and rocks, he might fall. However, with Randy running interference, I figured everything would be alright and it was. Randy led off and I followed behind on Bargain. We rode trails up one canyon and down the next. Once in awhile, he would dismount and get down to look at tracks.

"Cattle, like most animals, have a certain territory that they range in if they have plenty of feed and water. And they usually have a pattern of eating, drinking and resting. The catch is to find out where they are going to be at a certain time. We rode 'til about noon and ended up back at the truck. Bargain was getting easier to get along with all the time and he sure seemed to be tough. Randy's other horses were all shod but Bargain was still barefoot and I was concerned about his feet, but so far he was alright. We unsaddled and turned the two horses into the corral. Just to make sure they wouldn't bust out, we put hobbles on them. We also gave them some feed in the old grain bunk.

"We ate lunch, stepped up on the other two horses and rode out again. We criss-crossed the canyons on the trails we could find and towards evening ended up back at the corral. We were unsaddling when Randy said, 'We saw lots of tracks but no cattle.' Suddenly I heard rocks rattling on the hillside trail above the spring. We looked up just in time to see the bunch disappear over the hogback into the next canyon.

" 'Did you get a count?' I asked.

" 'Not sure but I believe the man was right, I think I saw six.'

' 'What now?'

" 'Too late for today. We're running out of daylight and the horses are tired, plus they have the jump on us. Tomorrow. I think I know how those cattle are running and I have a plan. We'll put the horses in the corral and give them hay and grain and bring along some junk tomorrow to fix up the corral.'

"We watered and grained the horses and turned them loose and let them roll and hoped they wouldn't break loose by morning.

"It was late when we got back home but Randy rumaged around and found some wire, nails, rope and tools and put them in the trailer. We also took along some horse shoes for Bargain. He also put in some hay and grain. Bonita and the kids had done the chores and had supper waiting when we got in.

"Early next morning we were off again. Randy also packed some camp gear and groceries and told Bonita he might not be back for a couple of days. He had done this before a few times but Bonita had finally put her foot down and he didn't usually go off like this unless someone was along. If he got in a wreck someplace and got boogered up, she wouldn't even know where to start looking for him.

" 'You never quite know how these deals turn out.' He said. 'That's what makes it so interesting, I guess. I have corralled a whole bunch in one day. Then too, I've chased 'em for a week and didn't get any.'

"When we got back to the camp, we started fixing up the corrals. We gave it emergency repairs and that took most of the forenoon. Then we caught Bargain and commenced fitting him out for a brand new pair of shoes. He didn't appreciate the kindness too much and we had to throw him down and tie him up. When we let him up, he ran around the corral whinnying. I didn't know if he was complaining or bragging.

"We had lunch and saddled up. Randy told me to go up the first canyon, cross over into the second canyon and scour it on down 'til I came out on the small flat.

" 'What are you going to do?' I asked.

" 'Stay here and rest 'til you get back.' He smiled.

"I was off on Bargain. Might as well get used to traveling with shoes. I rode up the canyon like Randy said and when I got to the edge of the pasture, I rode back down the canyon 'til I found a trail to where I could cross the hogback into the next one. Then I rode back up the fence lines, turned around and started to scour the canyon. I started looking for tracks and signs and as I got farther down I found both. I found a number of side canyons and draws that I scoured and I was worried that while I was up one of them, the cattle might sneak behind me and head back up but there wasn't much I could do about it. I just wished there was another hand along. I was beginning to wonder if I was going to bottom out before it got dark. I knew if I ran out of daylight, Bargain would likely find his way back to the corral where feed was waiting. But it was rough and rocky and I didn't relish riding in the dark. I also didn't relish spending the night out. I hadn't even thought to carry matches and it was getting cold at night.

"As I was running these morbid thoughts through my mind, I heard a clatter ahead of me and Bargain's ears snapped forward. I heard them before I saw them but we had jumped cattle and they were taking off ahead of us. Bargain sensed the urgency of the moment and the chase was on. We were only about a half mile from the corral at the time but I didn't know it. I didn't have any way of knowing where we were going so I just tried to stay on their tail.

"Suddenly we broke out onto the little flat. While I was gone Randy had parked the pick-up and the trailer beyond the end of the wing fence to the corral. He had strung a couple of ropes to fill the gaps and hung some rags and cloths on the ropes. It was a bluff fence. But it worked. The cattle ran past the spring and tank and were about to run around the end of the wire fence when they saw the truck and the trailer. They stopped momentarily and spun around to run around the corral on the opposite side but Randy was waiting behind a bunch of bushes and whooped them back. Just as they were about to completely reverse and head back up the canyon, I had caught up and they spun around again. Seeing the open corral gate, they no doubt thought it was an escape hatch and charged into it. We both galloped up just in time to slam the gate. A feeling of exhilaration spread over me and I am sure Randy felt the same way. We looked over the fence and sure enough, there were six head in there. A cow, a calf, a dry cow, and three yearlings.

" 'That was almost too easy.' I said.

" 'They're not in the trailer yet.'

"Suddenly I caught movement out of the corner of my eye. I slapped Randy and spun around just in time to see the last two head of cattle top out on a hogback and dip into the canyon on the other side. It was already getting dark and we saw their outlines against the skylines.

" 'Just when we were getting ready to wrap things up.' Randy said, half talking to himself. 'I wonder if there are more than two? They will be hard to catch. They either came along following the main bunch or were with them and ducked off. Either way, about the only way we will get them is to run them down and rope them. I am going to go into town and call Meddows to bring a trailer out and pick up the ones we have here so we will be ahead of the game that much. Why don't you see if you can make the shack habitable and cook up some bait. I'll get back as soon as I can.

"We unloaded the camp gear, lit a gas lantern and Randy took off. I got a fire going in the stove, put on the coffee and the chili that Bonita had sent along. I kind of swamped the place out, carried water in from the spring and put it on the stove to heat. We had all the food and utensils in big metal picnic boxes so the pack rats wouldn't be able to run off with anything. I also baited and set a few of the rat traps. Not that I thought it would dent the population much but at least it seemed like one was keeping even. I spread the bed rolls on the bunk beds and lay down to rest a bit after checking the fire and moving the beans and coffee to the edge of the range to keep warm. I had only meant to relax a bit but I must have dozed off as the next thing I heard was the pick-up pull in. Randy was back with word that someone would be out at dawn with another stock trailer.

"We were both tired and ate pretty much in silence and then turned in. It seemed like only minutes when the alarm went off. As Randy got the fire going again, I mixed up a hotcake batter and eventually we settled down to cakes and steak and coffee for breakfast. We had time to do up the dishes before the man with the trailer came. When he did come, we worked the cattle into the small corral and he backed up almost to the gate, then we parked the other trailers and pick-up on either side at the end to make a kind of alley way.

"At the last minute Randy said, 'Leave the cow and calf here. I have an idea we may need her. I'll bring them over when and if we catch the others.'

"To make sure she didn't bust out of the corral, we loaded her and the calf in Randy's trailer.

"We put some water and feed in the trailer for the cow and calf, then saddled up again and both of us headed up and over into the same canyon I came down yesterday. I had Bargain again. I don't think he had ever been roped off but I didn't have any plans of doing any roping anyway. I had done a certain amount of roping at brandings and some ranch roping and thought I was a fair hand but I could see that being a brush roper was a whole 'nother ball game.

"Randy figured that those two had been kind of running with that other bunch and would be in the same area. They might have been a little craftier and snuck out behind me. With two of us, we could cover the canyon a little better and hope to jump them. After that it was try to lay the twine on them.

"We rode for several hours, combing the draws and side gullies. Randy's horse had been through this before. Suddenly he snorted and poked both ears forward. A moment later the chase was on. About all I could do was try to keep up.

"Bargain had caught the thrill of the chase and he wasn't going to be left behind. We got glimpses of them on occasion and there appeared to be just two. Suddenly, they turned to the right and went right up the hillside to the top of the hogback and down the other side but Randy was right on their tail. As he went over the top, it was as if the earth swallowed him up 'til I also topped out and down we went. We went through brush, rocks, over draws and under limbs. I had been on a lot of tough wild rides in the arena and walked away from more than a few wrecks but that was the wildest ride I ever had in my life.

"We went up another small hill and as I topped out I reined Bargain in. I had a grandstand seat as Randy was closing in down below. The cattle came to a small clearing and made the break. Randy closed the gap and laid his loop on as pretty as you please right around both horns. He threw the slack over the hip and rode off as the heifer did a flip and landed on her side. It knocked the wind out of her and Randy ran in and tied her feet together.

"I thought, 'Here was a man who quit rodeoing because he thought it was too dangerous and then he goes off riding down wild cattle through this rough country that is ten times more hazardous than bare back riding. But such is life. I've seen men who worked high steel who said they wouldn't get on a bucking bull for a million dollars and vice versa.

"I rode up and said, 'Well, if there had been two of you, you'd of had'em both. Now what do we do?'

" 'We'll get this one to the corral first and see if we can use some strategy on the missing one. Apparently there were only two. If there were more we would have to ride'em down, but cattle usually don't like to be alone, although I have seen an occasional loner.'

"We put two catch ropes on the horns of the heifer which looked like a two-year-old. Then Randy took one and I took one. Bargain was going to get a little education on working a rope. One man can work an animal like this but if you have the room, two can do it better. We started the heifer down the canyon ahead of us and as long as she went ahead, we just kept up. If she tried to duck out, we had her by the horns. Sometimes they will 'sull' on you and you may have to leave them tied up for awhile 'til they get the notion to move again. We eventually got the heifer to the corral. We had to drag her in as she was not about to go through the gate by herself.

"The small corral in back of the larger one was in pretty good shape and we put her in there and then we turned the calf loose with her but left her mother in the trailer. After we fed and watered everything, the day was about shot. We were also damned hungry, as we hadn't eaten since breakfast. We took care of that next.

"Before dark, Randy moved the truck behind the shack and out of site and opened the gate on the big corral. During the night, the cow and calf started bawling at each other. Randy was hoping the noise would lure the other heifer into the corral or at least up close. Just at dark, he tied two of the horses up behind the shack and we put the saddles in the shack with us.

"Before daylight we were up and saddled the horses in the dark. If the heifer had come down during the night, she might be on the outside of the corral. When she spotted us, she would tail it for the brush and we would have a few hundred feet to catch her before she made it. Randy whispered that he sure would like to have the horses warmed up first but there was no chance of that.

"As it got light enough to see, we peered around the corner of the shack and there was our heifer, laying right up against the fence next to her partner on the other side. We let it get a little lighter and then Randy told me to ride out slowly to the back side of the corral. If we could, we would work her into the corral first, if not we would try to run her down. Luck was with us again. We handled her quietly and she jumped up and ran but when Randy jumped out, she hit the wing fence, spun around and ran into the corral where her partner was waiting.

"The rest was all downhill. We backed the trailer up to the gate on the small corral. The calf wanted to get to his mother and the two heifers ran in behind it. We penned the cattle to the front half of the trailer and put the horses in the back. We had a load but they were all in.

"Then we had breakfast. We loaded up the camp gear, cut up some firewood and put it in the box. We piled everything into the pick-up or tied it on the trailer. Randy said he would come back in a few days to see if there were any fresh tracks in case there were more that were missed. If it rained or snowed, then you had a good chance to check out this pasture.

"That night at supper we rehashed the whole thing for the kids and Bonita. Randy said he would start riding Bargain and get him to start working a rope. He wanted to give me a share of the money for catching the cattle but I refused. I knew he was having a tough time making ends meet and needed all the help he could get.

"I just told him, 'Hell, I was having the time of my life and besides I learned a whole lot down here. I wouldn't have missed it for anything.'

"Then he asked if I would stay on, as he got an order like this every once in a while. It was tempting. This had been like a vacation to me. I was far more relaxed than I had been in a long time and this could be real challenging but it was getting on toward Christmas and I knew I needed to go home.

"I had been thinking about if for a while and had almost decided not to go home this year. It was not going to be a fun time. We would not be gathering at the ranch this year, as Mom and Dad had moved into town to a small house. In fact, Christmas dinner would be at my sister's house this year. But I felt guilty about not making it back for the auction and felt I had better be there.

"I stayed a couple of days and helped Randy with some things that two can do a lot better than one and then one morning I was all packed and ready to go. I said my good-byes, shook hands all around, and climbed into the old Caddy.

"Randy said, 'If you're ever back this way, be sure to stop in.'

"I said I would.

CHAPTER 9

"As I drove up the road to the top of the ridge, I wanted to stop and look back but I didn't. I had a knot in my stomach. I was leaving a place where a man had made a home. He was going to work hard all his life to prove up on his claim but barring a bad accident or sickness or some other catastrophe, he would make it. And he started from scratch. I could have started a few rungs up the ladder and blew it. I took two days driving home and driving alone is sure mind expanding. Didn't even have the radio on much except to listen to the news and weather to see what the rest of the Nation was up to.

"I got in before sundown the day before Christmas and stopped at the filling station to ask where Dad's new house was. Turned out an old classmate from high school was running the station now and we had to visit some, even though he was closing up early for Christmas Eve. I found the house easy enough and pulled up front. The lights were on and I grabbed my warbag and went up and knocked. Mom answered and when she opened the door, she almost feinted. Then she threw her arms around me and started crying.

" 'Oh mom, don't do that.'

" 'Oh, I'm so glad you made it. I thought you wouldn't come. We hadn't heard from you for so long.'

" 'That you Buck?' I heard my dad's voice. "Well don't stand there and freeze. Come in.'

"Mom put on supper and we talked some of where I had been. I wanted to ask how the auction went but didn't know how to approach the subject so let it pass for now. I could tell Dad was not his usual self. He never really was very talkative but he had a wry, dry sense of humor and had little quips that he was always bringing up and if you weren't paying attention, you might miss the joke. In fact, I used to get the joke sometimes much later. Sometimes a few days later, when I would be thinking about what he said. No telling how many I missed completely. We got through supper with Mom and me doing most of the talking.

"Mom said there was a midnight mass at the Catholic Church and wondered if I would take her. Mom was something of a diplomat. If she said she was going and if I would like to come along I would have probably said, 'No, I'll watch the Christmas program on T.V. and wait up for you.' But when she asked if I could take her, what could I say. We weren't Catholic, in fact we had never gone to church much at all but my parents had tried to install good moral values in us and Mom read us Bible stories when we were kids. I had been to a few Catholic funerals so I wasn't exactly a stranger to a mass. Mom had said a friend told her there would be a beautiful service and lovely Christmas carols. Dad had apparently told mom he wasn't going. About eleven p.m., I cleaned up and put on my best western clothes. At the last minute, Dad surprised us and said he guessed he'd come along and keep us out of trouble. I was glad for the little joke as it was a sign his spirit wasn't completely broken.

"Mom was right, the service was nice. I didn't understand all that much about the mass but the priest preached a powerful sermon and the choir did it up royal with hymns and Christmas carols. Even ran into a few people who surprised me with their presence but I probably surprised them, too.

"We slept in Christmas morning. No stock to feed or chores to do. Dinner was going to be at sister Wilma's place, as they had a big house. She had married a grain elevator operator in a town thirty miles west. We ate a light breakfast in anticipation of the feast and piled into the old Caddy and took off.

"There was quite a gathering there. I had stopped at a western store on the way up and bought a whole bunch of red silk scarves. I gave one to all the nieces and nephews for going to the rodeos next summer.

"We had a big dinner and what with everyone talking, I don't guess that anyone noticed but me, that Dad had hardly said a word. After dinner, he went and sat in an easy chair in the corner of the living room and looked out the window. I finally went and sat beside him. I desperately wanted to talk to him but I just didn't know how to start, and the words would not come out.

"Finally I got up, put my hand on his shoulder and said, 'I'm sorry Dad, damn I'm sorry.' I turned and walked away. He was still staring out the window.

"Every time I had ever come home, I usually got in some hunting. There were deer, pheasants or something, and rabbits if nothing else. I considered myself a good shot with the pistol, rifle or shotgun. It was fun to get a few of the boys together and have a little hunt but sometimes I just took a gun and walked the creeks by myself. I shot a deer once with a revolver.

"This time though, I didn't stay. It was too depressing for me. I loaded up and headed south again. The Big Building Rodeos were on, the 'starvation circuit.' There is a lot of prize money up but the competition is fierce. Even the small rodeos would have a bunch of toughs. I traveled with a bunch again but I wasn't winning much and I had to borrow money for entry fees and expenses before spring. This didn't make me feel good at all. However, I knew old Buck wasn't going to make the finals this year so I started picking rodeos where I had a better chance of winning and didn't have to travel so far, and things started looking up again.

"I got my notes paid off and a few dollars in my pocket. I called home once in a while and found that Dad didn't seem to be doing so well but was getting by. Then, in October at a rodeo in Colorado, I got a message from the secretary to call home. I got Mom on the phone and she said that Dad had passed away. I said I would be home for the funeral. I checked the calendar and it was almost a year to the day that he had the auction.

"There was a big crowd at the funeral. I didn't realize that Dad had so many friends. As the family walked into the church, I caught a familiar face out of the corner of my eye, and though I knew it was out of place, I jerked my head sideways for a instant. It was Cindy, come to the funeral, and the hurt hit me again in the pit of my stomach. She still looked terrific but I had to pass on. After the trip to the cemetery, the church ladies had a feed in the church basement. Cindy was in the serving line. She was very much pregnant. I got to look her over a lot better then and she was prettier now than in her youth. We managed a little small talk as I went through the line. She already had a boy and a girl and we wished each other the best.

"After the funeral was over, the family and a few close friends went to mother's house. The talk got around to the past and some of the family wanted to drive out and see the old ranch and asked if I wanted to go along. I declined as politely as I could. That knot came back into my stomach. I would never own the ranch and I never wanted to see it again. I think the relatives considered me a little odd.

"That night everyone was gone except me. I told the rest of the clan, I would stay a few days to keep Mom company and after that some of the others would check in on her. We sat at the kitchen table drinking coffee. Neither of us was hungry. The church ladies had furnished a meal after the funeral but I doubt that I would have been hungry anyway. Mom started out.

" 'There really won't be much of an estate but there is one thing I kept back from the auction and I want you to have it.'

"She went into the bedroom and brought out a box. Inside was Dad's old Colt 45 revolver. The same one I had shot a deer with once. 'You were the hunter of the family and I know your dad would have wanted you to have this.'

'As I was driving down the highway again I pondered the thoughts of the past few days, the funeral and all. The death certificate said that Dad had died of heart failure but in MY heart, I knew he died of a broken heart.

"The rodeo seasons came and went and blended into one another.

"Then came Mom's death. After that there really was no reason to go home anymore, and no home to go back to in any case. The brothers and sisters all had their own lives and we had less and less in common.

"I wasn't getting any younger. Worse than that, I was over the hill as a bronc rider. I kept rodeoing because that was all I knew, or at least that's what I thought, but it was getting harder to make enough to keep going. I got to entering the smaller rodeos where competition wasn't as tough. There were getting to be a lot more rodeos in the eastern part of the Country and I made a lot of those although there were a lot of tough hands back there, too.

"The old Caddy was getting tired too. It was using lots of oil and it didn't have the zip it used to have. Then one day, four of us were riding into Nebraska to a rodeo when I heard something knocking in the engine. I looked down and saw the oil pressure gage drop to zero and I pulled it over on the shoulder. It was about twenty miles into the nearest town. One of the younger cowboys hitched a ride into town while the rest of us rested and waited. Eventually a wrecker came into view and hooked onto us and towed us on in. Two of the boys had stock up the next day and decided to hitch hike on in.

" 'Pick us up if you get that thing going.'

"Later on the mechanic looking at it came back wiping his hands on a greasy rag.

" 'I'll give it to you straight fellows.' He said. 'If it were a horse we'd shoot it.'

"The gist was that it had had it. He said he would take it off my hands for the wrecker bill and we could call it square.

"I guess I knew the day was coming so I said okay. The only thing I hated to leave behind was that set of longhorns on the hood. I thought about asking for them but didn't know how or any way to take them along. Hitch hiking with a bronc saddle and warbag would be tough enough. We had considered taking a bus but on examining our resources, found that we barely had enough for entry fees. We stood on the shoulder of the road 'til almost dark and thought we might have to go back and ask the mechanic if we could sleep in his Caddilac but just as we were about to give it up, a car pulled over.

"Time was when you could hitch almost anywhere and it wasn't unusual to see a cowboy on the road headed for a rodeo but in later years, it got tough to get a ride due to the hippies and the hoods on the highway. Usually when someone gives you a ride, he is looking for company but our transportation provider only asked us where we were going and then never said another word 'til we got there. He was kind of heavy with a dark blue business suit. Weird!

"The Contractor furnishing the stock for the rodeo was Bud Giles. I had worked some of his shows and guessed he was all right. I didn't win anything and was down to looking at my hole card. He was going on to Buff Springs next weekend so I approached him about getting on the work list. A cowboy that is pretty well known doesn't ask to get on the work list so it didn't take much figuring to know that I was a cowboy down on my luck.

" 'No I don't need anybody on the work list but we do need a judge. Can you handle that?'

" 'You bet I can.'

"I had never judged before in spite of all the time I had put into rodeos but everyone has to do that 'first time once'. I wasn't worried about the rough stock events but I would have to study up on the timed events a little.

"I ran into some cowboys who were going to Buff Springs and had them run back to where the Caddy gave out and pick up the rest of our gear, bedrolls and such.

"I rode along to Buff Springs with the stock and helped to make myself useful even though I wasn't on the work list. I managed to go along with the crew when meal times came and they didn't expect a man helping out to pick up his own tab so I got through the week okay.

"Judging didn't pay all that much but it was nice to pick up some cash after the rodeo. Apparently Bud had been paying attention as he said I could get on the work list next week if I wanted. That was kind of my beginning to get involved in all the stuff behind the chutes. Sooner or later, somebody gets hurt or doesn't show up and I would fill in. I flanked broncs, judged, and was pick-up man, whatever. Even clowned a couple of shows but that really wasn't for me. I was still competing and winning a few bucks now and then but probably only breaking even with entry fees.

"I worked off and on with several different contractors and eventually got over into Colorado and worked a few of Doc Steen's shows. I was on the work list again just doing the odds and ends. He had a livestock superintendent named Virgil. Virg was a tough-looking hombre. Had a scar down one side of his face that looked like a knife mark. He was okay but had a tendency to get mean and surely when he was drinking.

"One night at a rodeo in Utah, we turned all of the stock into the arena after the evening performance. Usually we watered and fed them and our days work was done. The cowboys, of course, head for the local watering hole to talk over the latest current events or to party. Virgil had taken the company pick-up and I went along. I am sure he had planned to have a couple of drinks and come back but he didn't come back. I was concerned about the stock and got a hold of one of the pick-up men to go hunt up Virg. He was getting pretty high by this time at the Shamrock Saloon. When I asked him about taking care of the stock, he bellowed back, 'F___ the stock.'

"I was kind of taken aback by this. He wasn't planning on feeding the stock and he definitely wasn't in any shape to drive even if he was. I found the boss's pick-up and as luck would have it, the keys were in it. The pick-up man and I took the truck, went back to the rodeo grounds and fed the stock.

"I was willing to let it go at that but somehow Doc had got word of what happened. Next morning at the rodeo grounds, I saw Doc talking to Virg who was nursing a big hangover. Next thing I knew, Doc whipped out his checkbook and paid off Virg right then and there. Then he got in his rig and drove off. Virg spotted me and came over.

" 'This is all your doing.'

" 'No Virg, you brought it on yourself.'

" 'I'll climb your ass for this, you son of a bitch.'

"I wasn't too worried about mixing it up with him. I had done some boxing in high school and where as I didn't have any desire to indulge in a pugilistic career, I always figured I could take care of myself. However, I didn't think Virg was the kind of guy to fight by the Queensbury rules. He was more of a barroom brawler. The kind that would put the boots to you if you were down. But when he called me a son of a bitch, I let drive with an uppercut that came from the knees and caught him right on the chin. He went sprawling and I suddenly felt sorry for him. What with that hangover and then getting rapped like that. I moved forward to help him up and apologize but he was tougher than I thought and he jumped up with a knife in his hand. There were a few cowboys around and one ran up behind and grabbed his arm and knocked the knife from his hand. He looked at me with the meanest looking eyes I had ever seen.

" 'I'll get even with you. Just wait and see.'

"I watched my back for a long time after that, especially when I went into a bar or honky-tonk but I never did see him again.

"After that I stayed on with Doc. He treated me right and I was eating regularly. I still rode broncs once in a while but I picked the shows where it looked like I could win a buck. Sometimes at the smaller rodeos, they might be short of some riders and I would take out a few exhibition rides. I liked that because I could pick my horse and then I could go out there and look good. But I got to riding less and finally quit completely.

"And there is your story about why I don't have a ranch. You're just looking at an old has-been cowboy who's future is behind him."

Sandy was sitting on the ground leaning back against a tree and looking down at her hands clasped in her lap. She remained silent for a while and then slowly looked up. She had a faint smile on her lips. She slowly got up. Came over and put her hand on my shoulder.

"I'm sorry it didn't work out."

The sun was going down and we climbed up to where the pick-up was. Again we took on the majestic scene and then slowly descended the trail back to town. She remained silent the whole way in and I couldn't help but wonder what her thoughts were but I didn't ask. In fact, I was perturbed at myself and I couldn't quite put it all together. Here I had unloaded my heart and soul to this woman and I didn't know anything about her, didn't even know her name. I guess I supposed that she would also tell me something of her past and about herself, but she hadn't volunteered any information and I hadn't asked. It would have violated the 'Code of the West'. She wasn't from the west apparently, so she wasn't bound by the code.

We got back to the arena just as the sun was setting. I was intending to feed the stock but found that Rick and Tom had just finished the job.

Rick winked and said, "Just thinking about the stock, Virg."

I laughed at that one and said, "Suppose this means supper is on me?" We went uptown to eat and talked mostly about the rodeo coming up the next two nights, Friday and Saturday. Mostly the talk was about who was entered and how it would go and that sort of thing.

CHAPTER 10

Friday morning dawned, the day of the first performance. No matter how many times, one has gone through it, it always made one a little more excited. It was an evening performance so we had plenty of time but we went over everything just to make sure we had it all put together. A carnival came into the fairgrounds during the night and were already setting up for the day. Doc and Marge came in during the forenoon. They had been back at the ranch to look after Floyd. He had apparently weathered the virus alright. Sandy helped out during the day whenever there was an errand to run or something to do and the evening performance went off without a hitch.

Saturday was a repeat and things went along pretty much the way Friday had. After the final performance was over, we all started to relax again.

"Another one down," Tom said as he was putting the horses away.

We fed and watered the stock and then I told Sandy, "Let's see if we can find something to eat."

We went uptown and there were still a lot of people around. The cafe on the main street was closed though, so we went to the club at the edge of town. The parking lot was full but we found a spot way off on the edge. We went into the club and the place was packed. A Country Western band was beating out a country song and people were talking, laughing, and having fun. There were all kinds of people in there. Some were local cowboys and contestants. The Pro Rodeo cowboys had already hit the road to make another performance somewhere tomorrow. There were also tourists and people who wanted to party. All the tables were full and just as the situation looked hopeless, a couple left a table in the corner and we hurried to it and sat down. We waited a long time but finally a waitress came to clean up the table and ask if we wanted a drink.

"No, not right now, but we would like something to eat."

"I'll be back in a minute to take your order."

Many, many minutes passed and I was kind of dozing off from the fatigue of the day and the noise when suddenly Sandy grabbed my arm and hissed, "That's him. Let's get out of here."

Her fingernails dug into my arm like a steel trap going off and I winced momentarily from the pain. I was instantly wide awake.

Now it's funny how a few years can change a man's attitude about things. When I was younger, my curiosity would have compelled me to stay and see who "him" was, but as one gets older, you get to be more of a survivor.

I jumped up and said "Hold on to me."

This was no time to be polite and she literally did hang onto me. She grabbed my belt in the back and ducked her head into my shoulder blades while I shoved my way through the crowd to the nearest exit. When we got outside, she broke loose and ran ahead of me to the pick-up. She went to the passenger side and I got in behind the wheel.

When I leaned over to open her door, she said , "The dome light." I took off my hat and covered the dome light and she got in, slammed the door and gave a big gasp and sigh of relief.

Up 'til now, I hadn't had time but now I was slowly getting mad. I knew it violated the 'Code of the West' but to hell with the code.

I grabbed her by the arm and said, "Look, if we're going to be friends, I got to know a few things. Are you married?"

"No I'm not married. Not here. I'll tell you later. Let's get out of here."

We drove back to the rodeo grounds. The carnival was tearing down and getting ready to move. I don't know when those people slept. I pulled up behind the gooseneck but Sandy told me to pull back by some trees and park in the dark. So I did. As my anger subsided, my hunger pains started coming back.

"I'll go over to the trailer and bring us back a couple of cans of beans. It's a damn poor substitute for steak but it looks like it will have to do tonight."

I reached for the door handle but Sandy grabbed my arm. "The dome light."

"Gosh, there can't be anybody out here."

"Please?"

She was really spooked so I had her cover up the light while I took a flash light, went to the trailer and procured the rations. I found two spoons, two cans of warm pop, opened the cans and came back.

"Now, let's get to the bottom of this."

"Okay Buck, I guess I owe you that. It's just that I haven't known who to trust lately but I think you are a friend. You may hate me when I get done with my story. But you were good to me and took me as I was.

"I was a small town girl from Ohio who was bored with the life I thought I was stuck with. I can't blame my parents for what has happened. They were both good people and good to me. My dad was an engineer and after my brother and I were old enough to go to school, my mother worked as a clerk in a hardware store part-time. We were comfortable as I look back on it but life was not very exciting and I wanted something more. I was considered good-looking, was a cheerleader, beauty queen, and all that, but my friends and I talked of becoming models, actresses and things like that. One of my friends had an aunt in California and after graduation, we decided to go there where the action was. My folks didn't want me to go but we went anyway.

"After we got there, reality started setting in. I didn't have much money and didn't want to continue living at my friend's Aunt's place although she said we could. She was married to a big, dark looking long-haired fellow and I didn't like the way he looked at me. I started hitting the modeling agencies but I didn't have any experience and wasn't getting anywhere when one day I found an ad, 'Models Wanted - No Experience Necessary.' I guess I knew what I was getting into but I was kind of getting desperate and I applied.

"It was a set up for nude pictures and they took me right in. I made a hundred dollars that day and actually they were very nice to me. I suppose they knew I was plumb green and were taking me slow for fear of running me off. I was, at last, employed and got a place of my own. My friend had gotten a job as a waitress and continued living with her aunt. My name was referred to other photographers and I was kept busy. One of my employers also ran a "Hostess" business where you could go to an affair with people who were short a partner and get paid for it. I soon got into that and started to make the party scene. Life was sure looking up. This was a lot different than Po-dunk Center, Ohio.

"From the hostess men, it was only a short jump to being a call girl. My conscience would bother me from time to time but I was having fun, wearing good clothes and getting paid for it. Still I knew that only disaster lay at the end of the road I was on, but right now I couldn't quit. My folks thought that I was modeling but I had already quit that.

"One night at a party I met a man named Vince Monticello. He was one of the most handsome men I had ever seen, black wavy hair and a smile that would melt your heart. I went with him a few times and he told me I was too good to be throwing myself away like this and would I let him take care of me? Apparently he didn't think I was too good to throw myself away on him. By this time I didn't care, as I guess I was in love with him and he set me up in an apartment. It was only later that I learned he already had a wife and two children.

"At first it was just great. I had everything I ever imagined I wanted. A fancy place, clothes, even a sports car. I don't know what kind of business he was in but supposed it was drugs. Soon he had me running little errands. I took packages here and there and picked up packages. I never looked, so I don't know what I was handling. I guess I didn't want to know. Although there were drugs all around me, that is one thing I never did, thank God for that.

"One day I met his brother and it was hard to imagine they were even related. His brother was a big fat man. Close to 300 hundred pounds and evil looking. He would look at me like I was shit but I think he was really jealous of Vince. He would make disgusting remarks about me, right in front of me, but Vince would come to my defense. They almost came to blows about it once. I was still doing currier work and even going into Mexico on occasion. I was leery of those things but Vince said it was okay, we had protection. Still I wasn't sure. I was getting nervous and started drinking pretty heavy. I missed a couple of appointments because I was too drunk.

"One day Vince sat down with me in the apartment and told me straight out that he didn't think that this was the life for me. If I ever wanted out and to go straight, he would help me all he could. But I stayed on a couple of more years, I guess I got in a rut. Vince was fond of me but it was a lonely life. I was tied up in that apartment way too much and when I was on runs I was uptight.

"Vince would take me out once in a while but it had to be discreet. He even got to talking about his family, and once when we were out, he showed me a picture of them. His wife was a beautiful woman, and I asked him, with a wife like that why did he feel the need to cheat? He jumped like I had stuck him with a pin. He looked off into the distance and never did answer me.

"But more and more I could see nothing but ruin at the end of the road I was traveling. I couldn't see how they could buy protection from all the law. There were City, County, State and Feds out there. And every time I made a run and got away with it, would up the odds of getting caught. Still it didn't seem to be the law but other gangs that caused most of the trouble. Every so often someone would turn up missing or dead. It really hit me when a guy named Sammy got it. I hadn't known any of the others and I really didn't know Sammy but I had met him a few times and had talked with him. He was a jolly fellow, one that was easy to like. I don't know what he got 'hit' for but it really shook me up.

"Then too, I had seen the other side of Vince. Like I said he was always good to me but I had seen him when he was as cold blooded as ice. One night he was staying at my apartment when the phone rang. I don't know what was said on the other end but Vince got livid. He cursed and swore and yelled, 'Kill the son of a bitch. Break his legs first.' He slammed the phone down and then picked it up and smashed it on the floor.

"It wasn't long after this that I approached him about getting out. I picked a day when he was in a good mood but I still didn't know how he would take it. But he was true to his word. He gave me a few hundred dollars and said I could keep the car. He said he could help me get a job but I said I would try on my own first. We said our goodbye's and that was the last time I saw him. I don't think I could have made the break on my own. I think somebody was praying for me, probably my mother and father.

"I called the friend I had come to California with and after a short talk to catch up, I asked if she knew where I could get a job. She was quiet for a moment. I'm sure she wondered what kind of a job and she finally asked.

"I said, 'Anything. Anything at all. As long as it's honest.'

" 'Waitress?'

" 'Oh yes that would be great.'

" 'Well you're in luck. I am expecting in a few months and you can take my place as I want to take some time off. I'll talk to the boss about it.'

" 'You're a sweetheart. I'll be right over.'

"I went to work as a waitress. It was hard at first. I really had never had a steady job. After I got into the routine of things, it wasn't too bad. I worked hard at it and got by. I moved in and roomed with one of the other girls. I knew I would be meeting a lot of new people and also men on the hustle so I bought a cheap wedding ring and wore that to stave off advances. I just wanted to be away from men for awhile.

"I worked at the restaurant for quite some time and when my friend finally came back to work, they kept me on any way. I worked hard and learned the trade. I was kind of proud of myself that I had sort of made it on my own and could learn to think and act like normal people do. I was a little apprehensive about leaving the 'gang' as they usually don't want anybody to leave. Anyone that knows anything and tries to go straight is always a potential witness. But as long as I had left with Vince's blessing I wasn't too worried.

"One day I got to work about five minutes late. Sometimes I drove and sometimes I took the bus and on occasion I walked. It was only about two miles to work from the room. But this day I took the bus and it got tied up in traffic. I got off the bus and ran into the restaurant. A man was sitting at the counter with the morning paper beside his plate. The headline glared out "MOBSTER SLAIN" and beneath in smaller letters, 'Vince Monticello was found...'

"I guess I fainted because the next thing I remember, I was lying on the sofa in the office with a cool damp cloth on my forehead and one of the waitresses holding my hand and talking to me. The boss asked me if I was alright and I assured him that I was. I got up and though I was kind of shaken, I went to work. But my mind was not on my work. All kinds of thoughts raced through my mind and about mid morning a call came for me.

"It was my roommate. She was coming in on the next shift. She was going to drive my fancy sports car to work and I would take it home. She was rather nervous. She said a man had come to the apartment door, knocked and asked for me, said he was a friend of mine. When I asked her to describe him it couldn't have been anyone but Vince's brother. Suddenly I was scared.

" 'There is something else,' she said, 'When he left, he went to the parking lot and looked over your car. Another man was with him.'

"My mind raced. If he knew where I lived, he would certainly know where I worked. I told the head waitress that I just didn't feel well enough to finish my shift. She told me I certainly looked ill and I had better go home and get some rest. I dashed out and went down the alley. I cut across several blocks and then a thought struck me. I ran to a pay phone and called my roommate. I told her I had to leave town in a hurry, she could have my clothes etc. and don't touch the car under any circumstances. It might be booby trapped.

"I only had about four dollars in my purse. I caught a bus to as far as it would take me to the edge of the city and started hitch-hiking. I knew that no matter what way I left, I was taking a chance but I didn't have much choice. I didn't care where I was going just as long as it was out. I caught a couple of rides, one with a salesman type who wanted more than to help a woman in trouble. He asked a lot of questions and I guess it didn't take him too long to figure out I was on the run. I got pretty leery of him and when he pulled up to a red light in a small town, I jumped out and said 'thanks for the ride'. He gave me a dirty look but the car behind him started honking when the light turned green and he drove off.

"Then I got lucky, I guess you could say. A carload of rodeo cowboys stopped. They had to make room for me but they seemed a cheerful bunch and full of jokes. They drove most all night and we got in the next morning to the rodeo where I met you. There were four in the car and I tried to stay awake to keep the driver company so he would stay awake. They took turns driving. They talked rodeo a lot but I didn't understand much about it then. When we got into the rodeo grounds, three of them were asleep and the driver said he wanted to take a nap. They had talked me into staying and seeing the rodeo although I was still not sure I was far enough away. Still, I thought I might catch a ride farther east if I stuck around. I thanked them and said I would see them later.

"That's when I ran into you and now you know why I came along with no luggage, no nothing. And you took me under your wing and I will be eternally grateful."

"But what about tonight?"

"I don't know. My mind wasn't working too good. The man in the bar was Vince's brother. I can't believe he tracked me this far. Maybe there are members of the gang around and one of them spotted me. I don't know how far out their 'empire' extends. Maybe he was just traveling through and happened to be in the club when we were. Maybe someone traveling through went to the rodeo and spotted me? I don't think he saw me in there tonight. But I can't be sure."

"Why would they be after you?'

"I don't know for sure but my intuition tells me they are. In the first place, I am always a potential witness. When Vince was alive I had some protection I suppose. But he's gone now. Maybe they think I had something to do with Vince being rubbed out. They may think I put the finger on him or something. And then..."

She was silent for awhile.

"Well?"

"Maybe he wants me for himself? I always felt that he lusted for me but didn't dare touch me because of Vince. Now Vince is gone."

"We turned in then but before Sandy went to the sleeper, I crawled up there and pulled out by warbag. Along with other things, I had put Dad's old .45 Colt in there. I checked it out and made sure it was loaded. Sandy wondered if he knew where we slept but I told her I would put my bedroll in the trailer by the door. I had two short chains with a padlock that I sometimes locked up the trailer with when we left it with saddles or gear in. I put them on tonight and felt we would be safe enough in the dark. Although it was not pitch dark as there were still some lights on the fairgrounds.

Anyway, it didn't matter much because I didn't sleep much and I doubt that Sandy did either. Every time I dozed off, I heard a noise, or thought I did, that would jolt me wide awake. A few times I cautiously got up and peered out through the opening along the top of the trailer but saw nothing. At the first pale light of dawn, I got up quietly and again peered all around. It was so quiet that it was hard to convince myself that there may be danger around. Maybe Sandy had a case of mistaken identity. Maybe the man was real but just coincidentally happened to be passing through and was unsure we were here. None the less, I stuck the old .45 in my belt just over my right hind pocket and slipped on a canvas coat that would cover it up.

We planned on loading out the stock this evening so they would be hauled in cooler temperatures and then tear down the arena on Monday. I would water the stock this morning and give them a light feed. As long as I was awake, I thought I might as well get with it. As I suspected, Sandy was awake too and we went out together and got into Big Red.

"I drove over to the arena and started running water into the small tank. The stock was dry and started crowding around it as they heard the hose running water into it. I had wired the hose up to the fence so the stock wouldn't knock it down, with the nozzle pouring water into the tank. Sandy was standing by the back end of the pick-up.

As I was rigging the hose I didn't see him approach 'til I looked up. It was almost like when I hunted deer. I would be on a stand someplace and watching to where you would expect to see the deer come in. But time and time again, you wouldn't see the animal come in, it would suddenly just be there. Sandy hadn't seen him either, or apparently even heard him and he was a BIG man. He looked like a 'heavy' from a grade B movie. He must have weighed 280 pounds, had dark hair, thin lips and a sun-tanned complexion. He looked like he had been up all night and he hadn't shaved yet this morning. Even his clothes fit the image. He was wearing a dark blue suit and white shirt. The necktie was missing. He was about a step behind her when I looked up and in the next instant reached up and grabbed her by the arm.

Sandy jerked sideways, turned deathly white, opened her mouth and tried to scream but not a sound came. My paternal instincts jumped into gear and the adrenaline started flowing.

He looked passed me as if I didn't exist and said to Sandy "You're coming with me."

"Hold on Buster."

I closed the distance between us in one jump. I grabbed his left arm but he swung it back and propelled me alongside the pick-up. He wasn't all fat and he had the advantage of weight. I would have fallen down but I hit the side-view mirror and it broke my fall. Then he looked at me with a contemptuous look.

"Listen, Hay Shaker. Take my advice. Mind your own business and you'll live a lot longer."

I went at him again and he dropped the grip on Sandy's arm and reached inside of his coat. I doubt that he knew that I was armed or he would have reached a lot faster. I jerked the old Colt .45 out of my belt and eased the hammer back as I brought it up. As I saw the gun emerge from under the suit coat, I squeezed off the trigger. At that distance I couldn't miss and I hit him just about an inch below the pistol handle. The gun made a roar like a cannon. I had fired that pistol hundreds of times in my life but I don't ever remember it making a noise like that. The bullet made a round black hole in the front of his shirt. Although all of this happened in a few seconds, it seemed like a movie in slow motion. There was a look of surprise and disbelief on his face. The pistol he was pulling out slipped from his hand. He opened his mouth to say something or yell but all that came out was a garbled groan, then he fell into a crumpled pile. Blood was running from the hole in his chest and some was starting to come out of his mouth as he was gasping for breath and then breathed no more.

The adrenaline was flowing and my mind raced. I jumped into the pick-up, started it and raced the motor a few times. Anyone in hearing distance just might think the shot was a backfire of the engine and not give it anymore thought.

The lines of a country song ran through my mind, 'I had but one chance and that was to run.'

But no. I had but one chance and that was to get rid of the body. I quick grabbed a hold of the man and tried to lift him into the back of the pick-up. Without a word, Sandy grabbed ahold and somehow we wrestled the big hulk onto the pick-up bed. I threw a tarp and some trash over him to cover him up. I had glanced around several times to see if he had any accomplices or if anyone was coming round but my luck held and no one showed up.

As I came around the pick-up to get in the cab, I spotted the pistol he had dropped and scooped it up. I threw it in the area behind the seat and threw a jacket over it.

What to do with the body? I knew we had to get rid of it so I started off the grounds on the road behind the barns where the 4-H kids keep their stock. Suddenly I saw the answer to my problem. Behind the barn was a pile of manure, straw and shavings from the pens where the kids kept their stock. A quick look around and again I was in luck as no one was around. Actually, most of the stock had been taken home the night before but there was still an occasional animal left.

I backed Big Red up to the refuse pile and feverishly dug a hole in the bottom of the pile. We rolled his body in and then tipped the pile down covering him completely. Then I looked at Sandy and myself. We were covered with dirt and blood.

"Back to the water hose," I blurted out, the first words I had said since the killing.

I pulled the pick-up up to the fence and took the hose and washed us both off, figuring the cold water was the best treatment for the moment. It pretty well done the job but Sandy gasped when the cold water hit her. Although the flesh should have been the last thing on my mind at a time like that, the picture of her standing there in those wet clothes is something I will never forget.

"You better get a change of clothes."

I wondered what next and looked at the ground. There was a big blotch of blood so I turned the hose on that too. Even though I muddied up the ground quite a bit, that red from the blood just wouldn't go away. It was like squirting oil on water. Suddenly a thought struck me. I grabbed a bucket with some grain from the pick-up and walked up to the arena fence to the walk-through gate. Some of the stock thought I had feed and started to follow me. I opened the gate and stepped back and a few horses came through. In a minute the whole bunch started following them. I walked back to where the incident happened and scattered some of the grain on the ground, the herd milled around the muddy spot and pretty well churned up the area.

With all the tracks there now, if a trace of blood showed up, one would just think one of the animals had got hurt and think no more of it. I hosed off Big Red. Luck was still running with me as no one had come around. I jumped into Big Red and raced to the motel where Rick and Tom were and banged on the door. "Quick, get up, the stock's out and I need help."

Yelling the 'stock is out' to a stockman is like turning on the alarm in a fire hall. In a minute Rick and Tom came running out, hats askew on their heads, shirttails flapping and carrying their boots.

"Someone must have let the gate open. I thought of trying to get them in by myself but didn't want to 'spill' them so I ran for help."

The stock hadn't strayed far, they mostly got into the hay pile, what was left of it. We loaded it up in the pick-up and I drove to the entry gate and into the arena. Since the stock was used to being fed from the pick-up, they pretty well followed along and Tom and Rick pushed the drags in on foot.

Rick commented, "Well that wasn't too bad. Remember that time in Carrington when the stock got out and went uptown? Things got a little western before we got them all back in that time. Hey, this has built up my appetite. We might as well go eat as long as we're up."

Right about then the thought of food churned my stomach. I said, "Look fellows, I am really not feeling too well. Why don't you take the pick-up and go back to the motel or eat or whatever and when you get done, bring it back. I'll go later."

"Okay." And they jumped in and drove off, probably wondering as they knew I usually ate a big breakfast. They probably thought that Sandy was still asleep and that I wanted to wait for her. They probably also wondered why I hadn't gotten her up when I discovered the stock was out but then would know that although Sandy was willing to dig in and help, that she wasn't a cowgirl and wouldn't be much help in a situation like this.

As the sound of Big Red faded away, the fairgrounds became deathly silent. I started back to the trailer. I didn't really know what to expect. I supposed Sandy might be crying or something and needed some consoling. I rapped quietly on the door and softly called her name but didn't hear anything. I tried to open the door as gently as possible but it always squeaked and groaned.

"Sandy?"

Again no answer. I looked around and didn't see her. Of course she might be hiding after a traumatic deal like that but there wasn't much of any place to hide in there. There was a certain amount of gear scattered around but a quick look around told me she wasn't amongst that. I looked in the sleeper and didn't see her in there. I even crawled up into the sleeper and threw the blankets back but she was not there.

My mind started racing again. Where did she go? Was she hiding someplace? Did Vito Monticello come out with accomplices and someone spirit her away when I went for Tom and Rick? Did she think that I had got scared and was running when I left? How did Vito get out here anyway? Surely she is around hiding someplace and is waiting 'til the coast is clear before she comes out.

I didn't know what to do next. I couldn't stay in the trailer. I felt the need to hide myself. Yet I felt compelled to return to the site of the killing. Something else might have dropped there besides the gun that I had overlooked. It was about one hundred yards from where the trailer was parked to the water tank. There wasn't much in the way of cover here to there. If I tried to duck and dodge on my way over, I would cause attention in case someone did come along. If I went straight over, I would be a sitting duck if someone was still around. Still I must chance it.

I started out slowly walking. Although I was sure no one was around, I felt like a hundred pairs of eyes were watching me. About halfway over, I stopped and looked all around again. Surely this was all a bad dream. I would wake up any minute in my sleeper snug and safe. I had never feinted before in my life but now I felt like I might. Perception was deceiving me. It seemed like my surroundings were getting smaller in ever widening circles like throwing a pebble in water 'til I was a giant and everything else was very small. Then the process slowly reversed 'til everything around me seemed very huge and I was very small and I was about to be crushed. Suddenly everything was back to normal. I was drenched in sweat and my legs were shaking. I wanted to scream out at the top of my lungs.

"Come on out you bastards, where I can see you."

"Sandy, where are you?"

But not a sound came out. As I steadied myself, I again started walking to the water trough. When I finally got there, I grabbed the arena fence and held on desperately. Got to get a grip on myself if I am going to get through this. Got to act like nothing happened. Got to be strong for Sandy. She is going to need all the help she can get. The thought of Sandy strengthened my resolve. I had to plan carefully so as not to pull a boo-boo.

I looked the ground over carefully but didn't find anything else. Anyone coming around would only see a muddy spot and animal tracks where the stock had apparently knocked the hose from the tank. I hooked the hose back up to the tank and let it trickle in, then turned my thoughts back to self preservation. I looked at my watch and the thought struck me. It was exactly a week almost to the minute that Sandy had walked past the water truck and I had seen her for the first time. One week and my life would never be the same. Another thought struck me. Maybe I would never see her again.

I looked around again not knowing just what to do. I couldn't hide as Rick and Tom would eventually come back. I needed to get into a position where I could get my back against something and where no one could sneak up on me. I doubted that anyone was around anymore or they would have made a play by now but my nerves were tight as fiddle strings and I was jumpy. I heard the sound of a vehicle coming. Was it a law man? Had someone heard the shot and called the police and they were just now getting around to checking on it?

As the vehicle came into view, I breathed easier. It was a pick-up pulling a stock trailer. Someone was coming to the barn to pick up a 4-H animal or something. As the truck drove slowly by, a man waved as country folk do, even though they don't know you. A woman and small boy were with him. I assumed his wife and child. They stopped by the manure pile where Vito was so recently buried. Surely they would discover him. But they only disappeared into the barn and came out with a Hereford Heifer and loaded her into the trailer. They left going around to the other side of the barn so I didn't have to wave again. Uptown I heard a church bell ringing. The local people were going to their Sunday services unaware that there had been a killing.

I went back to the trailer, not knowing where else to go. I figured that Sandy would come back there, too. An occasional car or vehicle would come out to the grounds to some of the stands or buildings picking up exhibits and such.

At last I heard the familiar noise of Big Red coming back. Rick was driving it and he came up to the trailer. "Tom is checking out of the Motel and fueling up his tractor. I am going to take mine down to the truck stop and fuel it up. Doc figured we could take down a good part of the arena this evening and finish loading up in the morning. See you."

It was a long day. Normally I would have taken the time to catch up on my sleep but rest was out of the question. I tried to get a grip on my thoughts. I wondered if I should have called the law. After all it was a clear-cut case of self defense but I wasn't too worried about that. I was worried about revenge from the underworld. If Vito was working alone here, I might squeak out of this yet, but if I turned this over to the law, everyone would know who knocked off Vito. I would be a marked man.

Then there was Sandy to think about. No, I had done the right thing. I just hoped we could get away from here before the body was discovered. It was a good thing it was Sunday as most of the clean up wouldn't begin 'til Monday. But then, if there was someone with Vito and I had been seen killing him, I was still a marked man.

I wasn't hungry but I knew I should eat something. I finally got out the camp stove and made some coffee. I opened a can of peaches and ate those with a few crackers. I didn't feel like going uptown and I wanted to be there in case Sandy showed up.

About four p.m., Rick and Tom showed up with the 'Pots' and I was glad to have company. Floyd was with them and we moved all the stock into the pens and sorted them for loading. We used a portable ramp set-up inside the end chute and loaded out both rigs. I am sure they wondered where Sandy was but they observed the Code of the West and never said a word.

It wasn't too uncommon for women to come and go in rodeos. Rodeo cowboys were forever picking up women and these relationships were anything from one night stands to going down the road together. Some got married for a while and some forever. But it wasn't unusual to see someone with a change of partners. Now if some young cowboy got dumped by a buckle bunnie, he was sure to get a razzing from his contemporaries but perhaps in deferment to my age and the looks that I was taking it pretty hard, no one mentioned it. I was glad that Doc and Marge weren't around. Doc wouldn't say anything but it seems that women aren't bound by the 'code' near as much, and Marge would have come and asked me what happened between Sandy and I.

After the stock was loaded out Floyd and I started taking down the arena and chutes. We had loaded what we could but Doc had said that he would have some help out here on Monday morning. We worked 'til dusk and Floyd said it must be supper time. I knew I should eat but still was not hungry. I told him to take the pick-up and I would stay. I went back to the trailer and opened a can of beans and managed to get them down. Floyd would sleep in the cab of his truck.

I decided not to stay in the trailer. I made up a bedroll and spotted a place under the grandstand where I would sleep. I waited 'til dark, so no one could see where I went, 'til I carried my roll and bedded down. However, I could have just as well stayed up as I got very little sleep. Each time I was about to drift off, some noise would jerk me awake. I had taken the old .45 with me and kept it under my pillow. I also put a handful of cartridges in my pocket although I don't know what for. I would most likely not get a chance to do any reloading anyway.

I wasn't sleeping anyway and at the first hint of light, I got up and rolled my bed. There was not a sound on the grounds and I carried the roll back to the trailer. I knocked softly and called Sandy although I knew in my heart I was not going to hear an answer. I softly went in and looked around but of course nothing had changed.

Floyd had parked Big Red by the trailer and I started it up and drove it to where his truck was parked and banged on the door.

"Breakfast time."

I was getting gant but still didn't have an appetite. I knew I had to start eating though, and after a bit Floyd came out and we went up to the truck stop for breakfast. I am sure that Floyd would have liked to sleep longer but he didn't say anything. In fact, you never really got into a heavy conversation with Floyd. He was strictly a nuts and bolts character. Talking with Rick and Tom was a lot more interesting. Rick was always full of fun and always had a joke or funny story to tell. He never got very serious. Tom, on the other hand, took life a lot more serious and one could talk about almost anything with him, from politics to religion and even if you didn't agree with him, it was always interesting. With Floyd it was strictly nuts and bolts. You could talk about the weather or cows or trucking but if you got into anything very heavy, his eyes kind of glazed over and he got pretty silent.

He had been married once but his wife ran off with a UPS driver. He never talked about it and I didn't know where his kids were. He would get on a bender once in a while and I think maybe that's why he took a ranch job so he would be away from town and temptation. Still, on this morning, it was good to have some company and I sure didn't feel like any heavy conversation myself so we talked about loading the chutes and stuff like that. He was going to take them back to the ranch and I would go on to the next rodeo. We had plenty of time so I ate slowly as my gut was still rebelling, but I got the food down.

We went back to the fairgrounds and waited for the crew that would give us a hand. They didn't show up 'til eight. A big front end loader appeared and we loaded the chutes. A couple of extra hands came and helped us load the rest of the stuff and at ten a.m. we were ready to roll. I said goodbye to Floyd and said I would see him again in a few weeks. I had the trailer loaded and was ready to go except for the pick-up horses, which I now loaded. I took one last look around the grounds. A clean-up crew was already working the grounds. I started up Big Red and slowly pulled off the grounds onto the highway.

It was a great relief to be on the road and heading to the next spot and I tried to make sense out of all that had happened but all I got was a bunch of questions.

How did Vito get to the grounds?

Did he have someone drop him off? That didn't seem likely as he would have had to have some transportation away from there. I figured someone else must have dropped him off and was perhaps parked not far away but out of sight. He was going to pick up Sandy and they would be on their way. When the plans went awry, the other fellow panicked and fled.

What, then, about Sandy?

Did he abduct her first and then flee? Or did Sandy perhaps know him from former days and they left together. Or did Sandy panic and just take off running like when she ran into me? But then why didn't she try and contact me? Or did she feel that she was exposing me to danger by being with me and decided to try and hide alone?

I had no answers to all these questions but was quite sure somebody must know. I had done in Vito Monticello. The underworld had a code too and somewhere, somehow, someone would be out to settle the score. It was a terrible feeling to be hunted and more terrible yet, not to know the hunter.

With the lack of sleep, I should have been fighting to stay awake but my nerves were still tight. Every car that pulled up behind me and finally passed could be a hit man. Would they try and run me off the road or would they try and shoot me as they drove by? I had put my .45 loaded on the seat next to me and threw my jacket over it. I didn't know what the law was in this region so in case a highway patrol would pull me over, I would have to throw it under the seat. I made sure I stayed within the speed limit so this wouldn't happen. I made up my mind that I wouldn't be run off the road. After all I had more weight and if a car rammed me, I would try to ram back. If they tried shooting it out, I would shoot back. Having made up my mind about that, I felt more relaxed.

The miles went by and I eventually arrived at the next rodeo grounds. I would have liked to quit and gone into hiding but if Sandy were ever to find me, I had to keep on so she would know where to look.

I pulled into the rodeo grounds. Rick and Tom had everything under control. Tom had been delegated to go haul some livestock so Rick was holding down the fort. He had already found himself a little 'honey' so he wasn't lonesome. We unloaded the pick-up horses and gave them their feed. I parked the trailer and we used Big Red to feed the stock. Then we all went uptown to eat. I hadn't eaten since breakfast and though I thought I was hungry, I still had a hard time finishing my supper.

We didn't have too many rodeos left for the season but I now developed a pattern for survival. I didn't sleep in the sleeper anymore. I made up a bedroll and would wait 'til it was dark. Then I would take the roll and go sleep out someplace that I had spotted during daylight hours, trying to pick a different spot each night. I tried not to have a set schedule and took my meals at different times. As much as possible, I traveled a different route when I went to eat or on errands although that wasn't always easy to do. I got to watching my back as much as possible. At the rodeo performances, that wasn't too hard and fortunately I didn't have to 'pick up' any of the others. As chute boss there was always plenty of cowboys in the rigging alley. The only time I was under the spotlight was during introductions but I didn't think anyone would pick me off right in the middle of the arena. Still, I always felt prickly when I was introduced and rode out.

Many times I would look out and thought I saw Sandy in the audience but it always turned out to be a stranger.

I got to looking at that pistol of Vito's that I had. It was a foreign made nine millimeter. It was a lot more compact and easier to carry gun than the .45 so I bought some ammo for it and started to pack that with me. When I had the chance, I would go into the country and do a little target practicing and I eventually got almost as good with it as the old .45.

As luck would have it, it was several days before the body of Vito was discovered. Apparently the manure piles were the last thing on the cleanup list but the body got to stinking and somebody thought an animal had died and was buried in there. Actually it was an animal.

The story in the newspaper told about a body found on the fairgrounds. It was in pretty bad shape by that time. It took a few more days before they could identify it and by that time, the law figured it was mob related. I felt a little better about that but it didn't change things too much where I was concerned.

When I went uptown I learned other survival techniques. Although most of the rodeos left were in comparatively small towns and it would be hard to tail someone without the party knowing it, I would drive around blocks and duck back through one alley and head back the same way I came in, things like that. When I went to a cafe to eat, I tried to go with other people and then would always try for a corner table or booth with my back to the wall and preferably where I could see who was coming in the door. As we were mostly in ranching country, it was easier because you could tell the difference from the ranching type and the country folks. Still it was a constant strain. And I got very little sleep. In fact, I didn't know one could get along so well with so very little sleep 'til I got into this mess. It would take me a long time to get to sleep and any unusual noise would wake me up. And on the fairgrounds and rodeo grounds, there is always noise. After a few hours of fitful sleep, I would wake up from something or other and hardly ever get back to sleep. And my sleep was usually filled with nightmares and bad dreams. The dream kept reoccurring of my walking down a country road and seeing a woman walking ahead of me. As I ran and tried to catch up to her, she would turn around and it would be Sandy. Then she would scream and run away and disappear.

CHAPTER 11

We finally wound up the last rodeo of the season and took all of the stock and gear back to the ranch. The stock was turned out to pasture after sorting off the stuff that was going to be culled out and go to market. Tom and Rick would be hauling stock with the 'Pots" for awhile, as it was Fall and there would be lots of cattle going to market or feed lots or whatever. Later on, Tom would go back to his place in Utah and Rick would work part-time in a feed lot and haul an occasional load of cattle. Floyd, Rod and I would do what had to be done on the ranch for the winter. We ate our meals in the ranch house and it sure was good to eat Marge's home-cooked meals.

It was good to be back on the ranch and I finally started to relax, and the second night in the bunkhouse was the first good night's sleep I had since the shooting. I wasn't worried too much about anyone sneaking into the remote place and if they did, the dog would raise a ruckus. Still, I was pretty wary and would keep my distance when an occasional stranger would show up at the ranch. They were usually hunters who got turned around or whatever, and of course they were carrying rifles. Whenever I rode out, I stayed off the trails and ridges. I would scout the draws before riding through and was always looking for tracks. After snows came in, that was a lot easier.

We gathered up the cow herd before winter set in and sorted off the cattle for market. Doc could still sit a good saddle and Rick, Tom, Floyd and myself got all the stock into the trap pastures connected to the corrals.

There was a big annual feeder calf and yearling sale at the local livestock center and the day before the sale, Tom and Rick loaded up the 'Pots' and hauled the stock to town. This is usually considered a holiday for the hands and most ranchers and the help look forward to going in and seeing what the stock brings and how the market is and all that stuff. For the help it is mostly a chance to visit and talk to other hands from various ranches and for some, a chance to party and hang one on. Tom and Rick had their orders on how to sort and pen the stock so Doc and Marge wouldn't be going in 'til the morning of sales day.

At breakfast, sales day morning, even Rod showed up with a clean shirt and jeans and a fresh shave, although he didn't have much for whiskers. It was just understood that we were all going to town, so Doc was a little surprised when I said, "I think I'll stay home today Doc. I am not real sure we got that south pasture cleaned out. I think I'll ride that fence today and see if anything got missed." I'm not sure I fooled Doc any but he said ok. He asked if there was anything I wanted from town so I gave him a short list.

As soon as they were gone, I saddled up. I felt a lot more secure on the ranch but it had got to growing on me, that if someone were really out to get me, there were all kinds of opportunities here, too. Someone with a high-powered rifle and scope could sit out where I would be apt to come along. One shot and it would be all over.

I decided to ride the ranch today and look through the eyes of a hunter instead of the hunted. Where would I go or wait if I wanted to pick off someone? I also kept a wary eye out because if I was on somebody's hit list, he would probably expect me to be in town today to the sale and figure it would be a good day to case the ranch. Of course if he were a professional like Tom Horn, I wouldn't have a chance anyway. However, I didn't think those city types would have the guts and fortitude to lay out on a cold ridge for days and nights waiting for his prey to come along like Tom Horn. And I probably wouldn't even be safe around the buildings.

Up in old Montana, Kid Curry had crawled up to shooting distance during the night and waited 'til old man Winters came out of his house in the morning on his daily trip to the out house. Kid waited 'til he was halfway there and then gut shot him so he would die slow and terrible. And he did, lying there and moaning all day. The few hands on the ranch didn't dare go out for fear that the Kid was still out there and they would get plugged too, although, no doubt, the kid snuck off as soon as he had committed that cold-blooded murder.

These thoughts ran through my mind and I thought about it every morning when I opened that bunkhouse door. It would be easy for someone to come up through the trap pasture behind the barn and slip right into the barn. Of course old Ruff, the dog, would surely detect a stranger's presence but there are even ways for a professional to neutralize a good watch dog. I got to carrying a treat away from the table at night and every morning I would give it to Ruff at the bunkhouse door. I just felt better knowing he was there on the job.

The job during the winter wasn't too bad if the weather was good. Floyd and I would feed the stock and we were usually done by noon. Occasionally I would ride out and check on the horses and if there was one that was losing weight, I would get it back to headquarters for extra care. If the weather was bad though, it might take us all day to feed. It was partly a job to keep us on the payroll 'til spring and I began to feel a little guilty because I had about made up my mind that I wasn't going to the rodeos this coming season. That would be just where a hit man would be looking for me and I planned on a change of geography.

I thought I better square with Doc so he would have time to look for someone else. He had been square with me and I owed him that. I was kinda waiting for the right time though and didn't quite know how to approach him on it when the situation took care of itself.

One night, Doc passed away in his sleep. He had been to a rodeo committee meeting and got in late at night or early in the morning and went to bed. He never woke up. I guess Marge could have run the outfit, but she said it just wouldn't be the same without Doc and decided to sell out and move to town. I told her I would stay on and help out all I could.

Doc had a big funeral as was expected, since he was well-liked and respected. Many of the rodeo fraternity came by to pay their respects as well as the local ranchers and neighbors. Although I felt honored to be chosen as one of the Pall Bearers, I would a lot rather been as inconspicuous as possible, mixed in with the crowd. Here I was right up front in the church in plain sight of everyone. Still I didn't think anything would happen to me in a gathering like this. Anyway how could I refuse? When Marge asked me, with those sad eyes, I would have said yes if it meant a death warrant.

She decided to have a bucking stock sale in the spring right on the ranch. She done all the promotional and advertising work and got that all set up by herself. She was a real trooper. Rick and Tom came back to the ranch a few weeks before the sale and we set up the portable arena and pens. These would go on the sale, too. Then we went out and rounded up the horse herd.

I will never forget that day. It was a bright cool day in April. The sun was shining and a breeze was blowing. There was still snow in some of the draws and coolies but most of the ground was bare. The saddle horses were feeling good and seemed to know it was a special day.

We found the horses in several bands and by noon had them all throwed together. Then Tom led off and Rick, Floyd and I hazed them into the home corral. I don't guess there is a more beautiful sight than to see a herd of horses running along with the wind in their manes and tails. The thundering hoof beats seem to fill my entire being. As the herd crossed the last ridge before coming down the slope to the gate of the horse pasture, the sun caught those manes and tails and it was pure ecstasy to see them spill over the top. There was also a lump in my throat knowing that this was the last time I would see this bunch doing it.

The date of the sale was early in May so as not to coincide with the big bucking horse sale in Miles City, Montana. Some buyers came a few days early kind of making a vacation out of it, but also to look the stock over ahead of time and learn what they could. They came from all over the United States and Canada.

The first day of the sale was almost perfect. The sun was shining and a light cool breeze was blowing. Just right I thought. Don't want it too warm. Want that stock to feel like bucking.

With all the people showing up, spectators as well as buyers and lookers, the old anxieties came back to me. I rather doubted that anyone would make a play against me with the crowd around. I couldn't be sure so I took all the old precautions. And kept that .45 handy in a gear bag with me.

The second day of the sale was warmer but still very nice. The stock bucked well and they brought good prices. Most of the stock was loaded out right after the sale but some was left 'til the next day and we got those out then. And then it was all over.

A stillness came over the place. The confusion and excitement was gone and suddenly I felt more lonely than I had ever been before. I had got to know all those bucking animals, especially the horses. Each was an individual with its own quirks and ways. I didn't realize 'til that moment how attached I had become to them. And now they were gone, scattered to the four winds. At least I had the consolation of knowing that most of them had gone to good homes and would still be doing what they best knew how to do, buck.

I looked around. Everything had been sold, the equipment and all. The arena had been torn down, loaded up and was gone. I looked to the empty space where the 'pots' and gooseneck had been parked. Even Big Red was gone. The lonesomeness crept into me like a bone chilling cold 'til I thought I was about to cry, when I heard the door slam on the house. Marge came striding out. She walked up to me and I knew she must be tired from the past few days and surely must feel this more than I.

I didn't know what to say but she spoke first, "This is no time to feel sad. I invited the crew into town for supper and that includes you. I'll see you at eight in the back room of the Cattleman Cafe. Why don't you ride in with Rod and Floyd?"

She spun around and walked off like it was the first day of the rodeo season. She had to be hurting but she was thinking of the crew instead of herself. Damn, what a trooper.

When I got to the bunkhouse, Rod and Floyd were already cleaning up so she must have told them earlier. I commenced cleaning up and was going to put on a conservative shirt when I thought, "Hell, Marge is right." I dug up one of the satin shirts I wore at rodeo time and a silk scarf. The works.

"Hey," Floyd chided, "You got a date?"

"Yup, with destiny."

Even though we kind of tried to buck each other up, it was a quiet ride into town. It was hard to get into a party spirit. I am sure Floyd and Rod wondered about the future. The ranch would be sold and they would most likely go to work for the new owners. But sometimes new ideas and things don't jive. Floyd drove slow, more like driving to a funeral than a party, so you wouldn't get there 'til starting time.

We arrived at seven forty-five and I walked through the front to the back room. The Cattlemen was divided into a front and a back. The front had a lunch counter with a row of booths on one wall and some tables and chairs in the center. The back room was closed most of the time but was used for special parties and gatherings or was open when there was a celebration in town to seat the overflow and things like that.

I wondered why we would be eating in the back room when there were so few of us, but thought maybe Marge wanted to be alone with 'her boys' just one last time. When we walked in, the first thing that struck our eyes was a big banner hung on the back wall that read, "WELCOME MD." The MD was Docs brand. I expect it was to stand for Marge and Doc and the MD fit right in with 'Doc", so it sure was appropriate. There were also some streamers hung around and I thought that was real nice. Marge was there to greet us and we all got seated.

She said, "You sure do look nice Buck," which made me glad I had duded up.

There would be seven, as Tom had his wife with him. Marge sat at the head of the table and as it happened, Tom's wife sat at the other end.

Rick came walking in at the last minute just as they were seating and exclaimed, "Sure looks like the women's lib done the seating arrangements around here." Rick, the jolly one. He never took life serious and was usually the life of the party. It was good to have him here now. He kind of got us relaxed and was off to telling jokes and stories.

Right off they got to talking about the incident on the last day of the sale. We had bucked out a horse called Blow Out. He was a good bucking horse but a little crazy. Now a lot of the bucking stock go through a personality change when they are hauled down the road. Some are a real pain to handle around the ranch but when we were on the road would give us no trouble at all. Others were just the opposite. Must have had something to do about feeling secure in familiar surroundings or whatever.

Anyway this Blow Out horse came out of the chute and bucked off his rider in about three jumps and then started running around the arena. Tom and Rick were having trouble getting him out so Tom built a loop in his ketch rope. Just as he was about to throw, Blow Out decided to jump the arena fence, so Tom let fly and roped him just as he was going over the top. Tom took his dallys and hung tough. I thought maybe they would tear the fence down as it was the portable corral panels we had set up for the arena.

Rick, without being told, galloped toward the entry gate yelling, "Open the gate."

Someone opened it before he got there and without missing a beat, he rode through and was also building a loop as he went through. He rode up and pitched his loop on Blow Out and gave Tom a chance to turn loose. They finally got the horse put away. The crowd got a big kick out of it. There was some joshing going back and forth.

Tom said, "Hell, I wasn't trying to be no hero. I just knew if he got away, we would be out there chasing him for about a week in that south pasture before we got him gathered up again."

There were two waitresses on our table and one was young and sure enough easy to look at. If she was married, she wasn't wearing a ring and right off Rick started trying to make points with her. We were getting relaxed and into the meal when a neighbor rancher and his wife came in. They came over and gave their regards to Marge, and Marge introduced them around to those they hadn't met. He said that he had heard that we were here and thought that maybe we could use a little company and anyways it was a good excuse for him and the missus to eat out. I noticed that he had a brown paper sack with a bottle in it in one hand. Now the Cattleman didn't serve drinks but sometimes they had parties in the back room where folks brought their own and they served the set-ups. I don't know if it is legal or not but they did it anyway.

It wasn't long after the first couple got seated that another came in and there was pretty much a repeat. And then another and another. Poor Marge would barely get a bite to eat but what another would come. The moccasin telegraph must really have been humming. We finally did get our meal down and by that time the back room was full. The waitresses were so busy that poor Rick didn't have time to get in half a wise crack, as quite a few of them had brought a bottle and they were passed from one table to the next, and the mood was getting pretty jovial.

When we got through eating, some of us got up and stood around in small groups talking. Down at the far end of the room was a juke box and someone went up and started putting in coins. Soon the place was throbbing with some good old country music. A few of the cowboys moved the tables and the chairs to one side and started dancing. There was plenty to drink and I was as relaxed as I had been since the 'incident'. I had only had a couple and I guess it would have been real easy to let go and hang one on. However, I had rode in with Floyd and I noticed that Floyd had kind of 'fell off the wagon'. I knew he had a drinking problem but he was in control pretty well 'til tonight. He was not going to be in any shape to drive home. And Rodreguiz was too old to drive. Don't think he even had a license. He drove the pickup around the ranch some but never on the road. So I cut it off after the two drinks and got a glass with some mix and ice in it and watched everyone else have a good time.

Eventually a slow song came on from the juke box and I walked over and asked Marge to dance. I don't know how old Marge was and I sure wasn't going to ask her but I guessed her to be a few years older than I was. Still, she was an attractive woman, not flashy but handsome. I had danced a lot at times, down through the years but hadn't danced for some time, so I felt a little awkward and self-conscious. But I didn't have to worry. Marge was a super dancer and she melted into my arms.

I had never had any trouble talking to Marge before and we were always quite frank with each other but of course we both had our 'places'. Now as we danced, the conversation should have come easy as 'equals', but I couldn't seem to think of anything to say. My mind drifted to other women I had danced with, to dances when I was young back home, where I knew most of the people and the dances in bars and honky tonks and rodeo dances down the road. At most of those, you didn't know anyone except the members of the rodeo fraternity. You dance with any likely stranger and sometimes wished you could stay around longer to get better acquainted but there was always that rodeo calling down the road.

Marge was wearing a subtle perfume that I hadn't noticed at first, but as we danced, it slowly worked its way into my senses. The person I had always thought of as the boss's wife was becoming apparent as very much a woman, and I wanted to hold her a little tighter but didn't know if I dared. Then the dance was suddenly over.

Before I could thank her, she said , "That was fun Buck. We'll have to do that again."

I did manage to get in a couple more dances with her but still couldn't think of much to say.

Everyone was having a good time it seemed. Rick was ROMPIN' and A'STOMPIN'. He was dancing with a pretty little gal in jeans and a pretty blouse that sure looked familiar. I took a second look and did a double take. It was our pretty little waitress. She was done working and had changed clothes and joined the party.

Later on we were joined by the local town cop and the sheriff and they seemed to be enjoying themselves as much as everyone else.

Through it all, Marge was the gracious host. And then, all too soon it was over. I found Rod arguing with an old cowboy about the merits of mutton over beef for a good stew. Together we picked up Floyd, who had passed out in a corner, and carried him to the rig. I drove back to the ranch to the refrains of Rod singing some old songs in Spanish. Occasionally he would break out in a coyote howl and then a cackling laughter.

We all slept in the next morning. Rod was up and puttsing around just like it was another day of the year although there wasn't much to do. Floyd didn't stir 'til noon and then nursed a hangover the rest of the day. There were the basic groceries in the bunkhouse and an ancient cookstove so I put together the meals for the day. Marge had stayed in town after the party, either in a motel or with friends and drove out to the ranch about mid afternoon. She was making arrangements to sell the ranch and then would move to town but would probably stay out in the country 'til it was sold. As she drove into the yard, she swung the station wagon over to the bunkhouse. She got out and called my name.

"I have your last check here, Buck."

"Thank you, Marge. I guess I will be needing a ride back to town but I am in no hurry. I don't want you to make a special trip for me."

"I do have to go in again in the morning. Will that be all right?"

"That will be fine."

I got up early and made breakfast for the crew.

"That's the last time you eat old Buck's cooking boys. After this you're on your own."

When Marge pulled up, I threw my gear in the back. I shook hands with Rod and Floyd and bid my good-byes and then crawled into the front seat.

Marge started the conversation by asking where I would be going but I really didn't know. I told her I would be heading down into New Mexico. I had kind of spread that story around to anyone who would listen lately in case anyone came around inquiring. I hated to lie to Marge as she had always been up-front with me, but self-preservation came first and if anyone came around inquiring about me, she would in all sincerity tell them the truth as she knew it. The thought occurred to me that if anyone was planning on my disappearance, I was sure helping him or her all I could. It brought a smile to my mind.

"Where do you want me to let you off, Buck?"

"Well I need a set of wheels. Drop me off at the car dealers and I'll see what I can find."

As I got out and hauled out my gear, Marge was about to say her good-byes but on impulse I said, "I would be glad to buy you dinner."

"Oh Buck. You don't have to do that."

"I know I don't have to but I want to. In fact, I owe you one. I insist", and gave her the best smile I had. "See you at the Cattleman at noon."

I couldn't help but notice at how her face had lit up when I asked her.

I looked over all of the used vehicle prospects in town and settled on a half-ton pick-up truck with a topper on the back. There would be a place to store my gear and sleep in when traveling. I bought a camper mattress to put under my bedroll and with what camping gear I had, I was ready to roll. I pulled up in front of the Cattleman's at a quarter to noon just as Marge pulled in with the station wagon.

"Well that's timing for you, " she laughed.

We went in and found a table in the corner and ordered. Several people passed by that we knew and said their hellos. I had always got on well with Marge but there was always a certain amount of restraint due to the employer, employee relationship. This would be the first time together as more or less equals. Of course we weren't equals, she had a ranch and I am sure was quite comfortable financially and I was a drifting cowboy. I wasn't exactly broke, in fact I had a few bucks in the bank but nothing compared to her. Still, the atmosphere was much more relaxed and we talked of many things that we would never have brought up when I was on the payroll.

Marge was probably a few years older than I was but was still a rather attractive woman in a subtle sort of way. I guess if I had been more of a con man, I would have approached her about running the ranch for her when Doc passed away. I might have worked my way into her affections and perhaps ended up marrying her and then I would have had my ranch, stock, contracting business and the whole caboodle. But it wouldn't have been the same. I would always imagine the cowboys saying behind my back, "Hell, he didn't earn it, he married it." So I passed on that one.

The price of pride comes high.

Anyway, Doc's boots would have been hard to fill. Still, I am sure she must be lonely but it wouldn't be fair to her either. I may be a hunted man and had already made plans to make myself scarce. Nevertheless, all those thoughts ran through my mind and it seemed I had never seen her as animated as that day we spent together. I even thought about changing my mind and hanging around but it was getting too far along for that. The stock was gone and soon the ranch would be, too.

We talked way past the noon hour and drank many cups of coffee. The cafe had emptied and was starting the afternoon coffee break when she looked at the clock and said, "Oh my, I must be going."

I paid the bill and we walked out to the cars. As we shook hands to say goodbye, she said, "Please keep in touch, Buck."

She took my hand in both of hers and I noticed her eyes were moist. I had to restrain myself to keep from hugging and kissing her and I guess if we hadn't been on main street I would have. As she drove away, there was a big lump in my throat. I thought I was too old for that but I guess one is NEVER too old for that.

CHAPTER 12

Now I must look to the future. I figured if Sandy had wanted to, she would have made contact with me by this time so I planned on hiding my tracks. The thought still nagged at me that she was out there someplace and just couldn't contact me and would yet, sometime and place, but I couldn't keep exposing myself. I planned on heading north but I didn't know if I was under surveillance or not. This would be a perfect time to make a hit as I would be leaving town and no one would miss me. To make it look like I was planning on staying over, I booked a room in a motel for the night. I even tried to sleep awhile in the afternoon but I was too keyed up to sleep. I went uptown at sunset and had supper. There weren't too many people in town and I was sure that no one was tailing me but I wasn't taking any chances. I went back to the motel, showered and shaved. It was now dark and no one was around so I put all my gear in the pick-up. I went back uptown to the bar and parked across the street. I went in and walked to the end of the bar and ordered a soft drink. I struck up conversation with the bartender and made 'cow' talk. During the conversation I again passed on the information that I was leaving for New Mexico in the morning. I hung around 'til closing time and then got into the pick-up.

The town was virtually deserted now. A pick-up load of drunk cowboys was the last to leave the bar and they headed out. I drove slowly back to the motel and then pulled out onto the old highway heading south. The old highway was the main street of town. The town was located on a river and a few years past, a bypass was built around town on high ground. The old highway, now called the River Road, ran north a couple of miles and then joined the new road. I drove south 'til I reached the edge of town, then turned down a side street, cut my lights and headed up an alley. I waited awhile and saw no response, so headed on north on the River Road about a mile and then again cut my lights and turned into a driveway. Again I saw no lights or activity and pulled back onto the highway and headed north.

I drove the rest of the night and in spite of no sleep, felt wide awake, the anxiety keeping me alert. Daylight found me in Wyoming. I suddenly felt freer and younger than I had in years. I felt I had shook the past and was ready to take on the world. Although there was no one to hear but me, I let out a beller and wha-hoo that could be heard in the next county. I really hadn't planned too much on where I was going so I really didn't know where I was at. I was also getting hungry and was low on fuel. I had some canned goods in the back and two five-gallon cans of gas so I wasn't worried. In fact, I was about to look for a place to pull off and grab a bite when I saw the sign Rock City, Thirteen Miles. I drove on in. Rock City was a motel, cafe, gas station combination. Population eleven. I wondered if the cafe would be open as some of these places were pretty much summertime deals, but there were three old beat-up ranch pick-ups parked in front and I turned in.

There were five rancher - cowboy types in having breakfast. They all nodded and said hello even though we had never seen each other before. Them folks were country and were just observing the Code of the West. The cook and the waitress was a middle-aged blonde who would have been pretty good looking but she was packing a few extra pounds. She was wearing a tight white dress.

As I strolled up to the counter she said, "Howdy stranger, what'll it be?"

I looked up on the wall behind the counter and the sign said 'Cowboy Special: Steak, eggs and potatoes'. I nodded and asked for the special.

After I had eaten, I asked if I might park my rig behind their establishment and take a nap. I figured I was less apt to be bothered here than parked out in the country someplace where someone would stop and ask if I was having trouble. The waitress-cook said okay so I pulled behind the gas station in a small parking lot. I crawled in the back and rolled out my bedroll. The combination of lack of sleep and a full stomach, the relaxation of leaving the past all came together. I pulled off my boots, lay down and hardly remembered my head hitting the pillow. When I finally woke, it took me awhile to get oriented and figure out where I was. My mind finally started to clear and I remembered that I was parked in Wyoming. I pulled on my boots and slipped out. The sun was just going down. I wandered back to the cafe. The same waitress-cook was there and the place was empty. I walked in and sat down at the counter.

"Some nap, I thought you had died out there. I was just getting ready to call the law." She had a trace of a smile on her face. "All that sleep make you hungry?"

"Yeah, I guess it did. What's for supper?"

A middle-aged man came in from the station. It turned out, he was her husband and they ran the combo together. During the summer, things got a little busier and they hired help but they ran it alone during the winter. We talked about the country, the weather and cattle prices. After I finished eating, I filled up the pick-up with gas and headed north.

I bounced around between towns here and there a few days asking about ranch jobs and the like but not quite finding anything I might like. I finally drifted over to Boulder Creek. I rode there once at a rodeo and kind of liked the look of the country around there.

When looking for a job in a western town, there are several possibilities. The local feed store is a good spot. Also the saddle shop, although there are not nearly as many of those as there used to be. Time was when just about every town had a saddle shop. But the best spot is still the local saloon. The bartender always knows who got fired or quit or who's hiring, and when a rancher wants help, he nearly always tips off the bartender. So when I spotted the Long Horn bar, I pulled the pick-up over and walked in. It was mid morning and the joint was pretty quiet. I ordered a beer. The bartender looked familiar and it finally dawned on me who he was.

"You John?"

He squinted back momentarily and yelled, "Buck! Buck, you old son of a bitch." He grabbed my hand and I thought he would never let it go.

We hadn't seen each other for several years. John D. McCormick had been one hell of a bronc rider. He was older than I and was getting pretty gray. He had also put on weight like most folks do when they get older. He was kind of past his prime as I was approaching mine, so I never did get to know him too well. Still, we made a lot of the same rodeos and he helped me out from time to time with rigging my horses and tips about riding. He was championship material and probably could have won the World Championship if he had tried a little harder but he liked to party a little and if you were going after the World, you can't take out much time for that. He always seemed to have some good looking woman along when he was rodeoing.

I remember one rodeo where he drove up behind the chutes and this woman got out of his car. I don't know if they just came from a party or if they were going to one but she was sure enough dressed for one including silk stockings and high heeled shoes. And nobody joshed John D. about his women. He was about half tough and could sure take care of himself in a fight.

Well, John D. had kind of drifted away from rodeo and here I ran into him bartending. We talked for some time about rodeos and rides and things like that. It's one reason old cowboys take up bartending, so they can get to visit with so many of the old hands.

I finally got around to asking what the job prospects were and he said, "They're looking for an arena director for the Cody Nite Rodeo. You could sure handle that."

"Uh,... I was uh,... kind of looking for uh,... something kind of quiet and off the beaten path." I looked down at my glass and slowly twirled it with my fingers.

"Ooooh." He replied ever so slowly. "I see." He thought a minute. He just surmised that I was on the dodge, and he observed the Code of the West. You help out a friend in trouble and you don't ask any questions. "I know just the job for you. The Mile High Grazing Association is looking for somebody to ride the community pasture. They have a line camp up in the mountains and you would be up there alone all summer. Only guy you get to see is the camp tender once a week or so. Only reason he comes up is to see if you're still on the job." He smiled. "They don't care about you. They are worried about somebody looking after the cows. They can't get anybody to stay there more than one season. Too much like sheep herding. By the time those fellows come down in the fall, they are pretty weird. It ain't like in the old days. Hell, half those old time cowboys spent half their life in a line camp or out alone someplace. Can't get people to do that anymore. What do you think?"

I thought it sounded good to me and he gave me a name and a phone number to contact. I gave the man a call and he was sure glad to hear from me. He told me where to meet him and I said I would be right over.

I went back to the bar and told John, "It looks like a winner."

"Glad to be of assistance."

I turned to leave and then turned back. "By the way, my name is Will Jameson."

"Sure thing," and he winked as I left.

The man I talked with was Gary Wallen. He seemed to be the secretary-treasurer, ram rod or whatever of the Assc. He also had a ranch and owned a bunch of cattle in the pool. I thought he would be grilling me on whether I could hack it but he just talked about a lot of things. In retrospect, I think he was a lot more of a student of humanity than I gave him credit for at the time. A lot of what I thought was innocent conversation, was in fact exploring my abilities and attitudes. I didn't lie about my past, I just didn't put in too many identifying times and places. When he asked if there was any special reason for applying I answered", I need a job." He let it go at that.

Gary said he had something to do around town and if I wanted to, I could go out to the ranch. I wouldn't be going on the payroll for a couple of weeks yet, as most ranchers were not done calving yet. I could stay at the ranch though and help out as much as I wanted to take care of room and board. I said that was fair enough.

I followed Gary's directions and drove out to the ranch. The place looked almost deserted. There was a ranch house and a bunkhouse, barn and corrals. I looked into the bunkhouse but apparently no one was staying there at the time. I walked up to the main house and knocked but no one answered. I was about think I had got on to the wrong place and was even thinking of leaving when I heard a pick-up come roaring up the road. It pulled into the yard and up to the barn and stopped suddenly. The cloud of dust that had been chasing it now caught up, momentarily engulfed it and then drifted on by. A man in brown coveralls and hat got out and went into the barn. I started walking to the barn and was halfway across the yard when he came out. He hadn't seen me 'til then and I startled him. I went on over, introduced myself and stuck my hand out. I told him that Gary had sent me out but there didn't seem to be anyone around.

"I haven't got time to talk right now," he said. "I came up here to get a calf puller. I'm heading back to the other place. Follow me if you want."

With that he jumped into the pick-up and roared off. Well there didn't seem to be much going on around here so I got into my rig and followed. He went down a side road about three miles up over a rise and down a hill to a cow camp. It was situated on a creek. There were several big sheds and barns, some pens and corrals, a big flat that was no doubt irrigated hay grounds. Right now there were several hundred head of cows and almost that many new calves out there. Two mobile homes parked off to the side in a grove of trees made up the rest of the set-up. I pulled up behind where the pick-up was parked by one of the big sheds. There was a walk-through door there and I cracked it a little to see what was on the other side and then walked on in. The big shed was divided into a series of box stalls and the man I followed along with another fellow were in a pen across the alley. I walked over and looked in.

A heifer was laying on her side. Two small feet were protruding from her rear end and the man with the brown coveralls was already attaching the calf puller. It was a case of too small a heifer and too big a calf. After about twenty minutes of careful winching, the heifer let out a beller and the calf came sliding out. The calf was alive but kind of weak from the ordeal. The heifer didn't look any better. They rubbed the calf down and then drug him over to the heifer who was still lying down. They stuck a finger in its mouth and when he started to suck on it, they squirted milk in his mouth. The taste of the warm milk got his saliva to working and he sucked and slobbered and then tried to get up. When the two fellows figured they had got enough milk in him to last awhile they left them to rest.

"I think they'll make it now," the man in the brown coveralls said. "By the way, my name is Bill Hanson. I guess I'm the foreman here. This is Slim Wilkins. He is the only other man here, so if he quits, I'm without a crew. We have been calving out this herd for almost two months and NOW the boss sends out another man when we're about done!"

"My name is Will Jameson and I'm afraid you haven't gotten another man yet. I am going to be the pasture rider in the Grazing Assn. Community Pasture.

There was silence for awhile, then Bill said, "Well hell, you might as well come in and have some coffee."

We went to the bigger of the two trailers which I was to find out eventually was the home of Slim and his wife Gwen. They had two pre-school kids. Under the arrangement of their employment, she did the cooking for the crew, when there was one. At this time she cooked for Slim and Bill. Bill was a bachelor and took his meals with them.

I detected a very cool reception from both of the men. I put it off to the fact that they had been calving for almost two months and that can be a grinding routine under the best of circumstances and grueling under adverse conditions.

Back at Doc Steen's ranch, it wasn't all that bad. Doc calved later than most ranches and let his cows calve out in the pastures. We checked them once a day when we took out feed or cake and they pretty well took care of themselves. Occasionally one would need help or we guessed that a calf hadn't sucked and we would rope the cow to get the calf on her, but most of the time we let nature take its course.

In the old days of open range, the cattlemen just let the stock run and there really wasn't much herd or range management. But in those days most of the big outfits ended up with about fifty percent calf crop. Sixty percent was considered good. After a combination of the west settling up and several bad winters put most of the big outfits out of business, the smaller ranches started winter feeding, breeding up the livestock and taking better care all around or you couldn't stay in business.

Today cowmen try for one hundred percent but feel pretty lucky if they get ninety five percent calf crop. I did know one small cowman though who bragged that he got over one hundred percent several different years. He ran a good operation and had a few cows that dropped twins. To do this means that you kind of have to 'live with those cows' during calving time. Most all ranchers do this especially if the weather gets bad. It means the cows must be checked pretty regular.

We had sat down to coffee and rolls. Slim had introduced me to his wife and we sat there in a kind of awkward silence.

I figured maybe now was a time to make points. After all Gary had said I could work as much as I wanted to earn room and board. I hadn't figured on working very hard but I thought I would offer my service anyway.

I broke the silence with, "I don't know what kind of schedule you fellows have been keeping but I expect you're getting kind of short on sleep. Why don't you show me what has to be done and I'll take the night shift. Give you guys a chance to get a good night's sleep."

They both darted a quick look at each other and an immediate change came over the atmosphere. Slim responded first with a smile and then said to Bill, "Grab him quick before he changes his mind."

We then went out and Bill showed me around. They had been checking the stock every two hours. They took turns so it wasn't too bad unless something needed help and then it might be both of them. Or if the weather was bad, the heifers were kept up in a lot beside the big shed where they had just pulled the calf. If one was really close up, she was put in a box stall inside. This evening there would be six inside. The remaining cows were in a small pasture next to the big corral. We checked on the recently-pulled calf and heifer and found the calf nursing.

We went on in to supper and Gary had made a good deal when he hired Gwen to cook. She was alright and it was good to get some home cooking again.

Bill said, "You might as well bunk with me. There is a spare room in my trailer."

We went on over and he fixed me up with an alarm clock. I would have to remember to set it up every two hours. I didn't have any trouble waking up as I was a very light sleeper since the 'incident' and I tried to be quiet as I went out to make the rounds, although I was sure Bill woke up every time anyway. He probably didn't sleep too well wondering what kind of new hand I was.

The night passed without incident. One of the heifers had a calf but it was already born on the two a.m. round and looked like it had nursed. At breakfast Slim remarked that it was sure nice to go to bed and not get up 'til morning.

The next few weeks went by. As I was bunking with Bill, he filled me in on the ranch and gave me some pointers on riding the summer pastures. Turned out he had put in some time up there himself. Most everyone that was hired put in the whole summer. Some just quit and then someone would fill in 'til a replacement could be found.

I was kind of surprised that Gary never came around and mentioned this to Bill one day, "No he don't come around much. He's a 'town' rancher. He hardly ever stays at the house." Then in a lower tone he confided, "I'm not sure that he is going to be able to hang onto the place. Kind of a shame. This place was in the family for a long time. His great-grandpa homesteaded out here and started putting this place together. Then Gary's dad sent him off to college and he learned how you are supposed to prosper in the cattle business. Then Gary's dad died and left the place to him. He had married when he was in college and brought his wife out here to the ranch. I guess it was kind of hard getting adjusted but she tried and was doing alright. I had worked for the 'old man' a few times and around on different ranches, and was working here when the old man died. That's how come I got this foreman's job. Anyway, Gary was forever running off to meetings and joining this and joining that and never was around here like he should be except when there was a building program going on. He seemed to like that. That's why we have all these buildings here and those pens and squeeze chutes and calf table. We artificially inseminate all the cows and that ain't all bad but I guess I kind of liked the old time way better. Trouble is he took on a lot of debt to pay for all this and I am worried that he ain't going to make it."

"Doesn't he have a family?"

"Oh, he HAD a family. He has a son and daughter. The girl is in Los Angeles. Don't know what she is doing. The boy went to college too and is a geologist I think. he ain't much interested in cattle. Every time he comes home, he tromps around out there in the hills with his little pick looking for fossils. I expect if Gary dies, he'll sell the place, (A pause) if the bank don't sell it first."

"What about his wife?"

"Oh her. Can't say as I blame her much. She would be out here alone and he was forever gone. Especially when he got to be secretary of this Grazing Association. Don't think there is much if any money in it but it gives him a chance to act like a big shot. Anyhow, he came back from one of those meetings and there's a note on the table and that's all there was to that. Don't really know where she went to." As an afterthought he said, "She was a looker, too!"

CHAPTER 13

Then came the big day when the cow herd was trailed to summer pasture. All the ranchers who had cattle in the pool trailed their herd up there and made a gala affair of it. In the old days, two and three thousand head herds were trailed north out of Texas or wherever and the crew was usually about ten to twelve men, give or take a few, depending on the country and things like that. Eight cowboys trailed the cow herd, one or two took care of the horse herd and a cook drove the chuck wagon. If they were going through new country, there might be a 'pilot' or scout up ahead looking for water and a good bed ground. When the cattle industry moved north, a bed wagon was added to the entourage to carry the bedrolls, tents and extra gear needed in the colder climate. But in later years as cattle got to be hauled more than trailed, folks got to make a picnic out of the few opportunities that presented itself to trailing stock. The cattle weren't as wild and everyone in the family joined in as well as relatives, neighbors and a few people from town who wanted to play cowboy. Some of the ranches even got to advertising and dudes would come from the east to come out and join the fun for $100 or so a day. And the way economics of ranching is going, this might be their only profit for the year.

Anyway, the herds were trailed to the summer grazing and some of the ranches threw their stock together and trailed them up. We threw in with a neighbor and there were quite a few riders going along for the fun. I didn't mind as long as they stayed out of the way. We took three days going up, as we didn't want to move more than about ten miles a day, due to the little calves. Some of the calves that looked a little weak were hauled in a pick-up. Again in the old days, the work wasn't done at sundown, somebody had to keep an eye on the herd all night to keep them from straying, but today, there was always a trap pasture to put them in. So the evenings were spent around a campfire singing and telling stories. And the food was great. One thing, the modern trail drivers ate a hell of a lot better than the old-time cowboy.

After we got all the stock delivered to the summer pasture, Bill stayed with me a couple of days to get me oriented to the new job. There was a base camp that could be reached with a four-wheel drive truck and the truck would bring my supplies and salt blocks, etc. to this camp. There was a small shack there, a metal storage building, a corral and small pasture. About seven miles up the mountain was the camp where I would spend the most of the summer. There was a cabin there too, a corral and fenced pasture there for my horses, with a creek running through it. My duties for the summer were to ride the big pasture and keep an eye on the stock and meadows. I was to keep the stock scattered out or if one meadow was being over-grazed, to move the stock accordingly. I would also be putting out salt blocks and I would have to pack all those around on pack horses. I would have six horses in my string.

Everything I needed at the home camp had to be packed in. I had never done any packing before but Bill showed me what I had to know and made the first trip with me. He stayed overnight, showing me where things were and we rode down the next morning. He helped me pack up again and then said, "Well, you're on your own now. I probably won't see you 'til the fall gather. The camp tender will come by about every two weeks or so with supplies and salt and if you need anything, you can leave the request with him. I have the dates marked on the calendar when he will be here so be sure to keep track of time."

I started up the trail with the pack string strung out behind me. About a half mile up, the trail turned and the base camp could no longer be seen. I noticed that Bill's truck was still by the cabin so he waited 'til I was out of sight to leave. I was alone now but didn't have the time to be lonely. I was new at packing and was anxious about the horses. I was left with six horses, two riders and four packers, although they had all been rode. They were good horses and I guessed that was only good business. You wouldn't want someone to get 'boogered up' in the high pasture all alone. Still, things can happen and I was to learn a lot more from my horses that summer than they learned from me. We had a few wrecks but for the most part made out all right.

I was pretty busy the first two weeks packing salt to all the places in the pasture. Bill had fixed me up with a map of the whole area with trails and places I should place the salt blocks and things like that. I was also making trips from the base camp with the salt, supplies, etc. Part of my gear was a 30-06 rifle with a scope in case I had predator problems. Of course some of those predators were supposed to be protected but Bill said, "Protect yourself first." I was remote enough that I wasn't apt to be bothered much anyway. Groceries was in the form of dry goods, canned goods and cured or canned meat. I would get some fresh meat when the camp tender came there. Although nothing was said, I think it was kind of understood that if you wanted fresh meat, you were supposed to go and get some.

I had got a holster made for the old .45 Colt and now carried it with me all the time. It just got to be a part of my clothing. It is one place where a cowboy still carries a gun when he is riding alone. You never know what you might come onto suddenly or if a horse should fall and you were hung up, you might just save yourself if you had a pistol handy. Besides a little target practice, I did bring in some small game on occasion to change the diet.

There were a number of fifty-gallon metal barrels at base camp filled with grain for the horses and they always got a feed when I went down. I sacked some up and took back with me each trip so I could give them some at home camp but they got very little up there. It did make them a lot easier to catch though. Some days, especially if the weather was good, I made a trip and a half. I would go down early, give the horses a feed while I was loading up, and take off for home camp. I would unload, grab a quick lunch and head back down the mountain. I could turn the pack horses loose and they would be waiting for me at the corral knowing that they would get grain there again. Then I would stay overnight and get an early start up the mountain again in the morning.

I was busy enough the first two weeks that I almost missed the day to meet the camp tender. I went down the trail the evening before and stayed at base camp so I would be ready to go as soon as he came in. He came in with the truck about ten thirty a.m. and we unloaded. He was a young college kid and took the job for the summer. Seemed like a nice kid but wasn't too educated in the ways of the west. I had a fire in the stove in the shack. I had the coffee pot on and a stew off to the side so I could have a quick lunch before going back up. When we got the truck unloaded, I invited him to sit down for dinner. I guess he didn't trust my cooking, as he declined, but he did nurse a cup of coffee. He asked if there was anything I wanted and I told him to bring me the old newspapers so I would know what was going on in the world and he said he would.

I had him help me pack up before he left. He didn't know anything about packing but he was young and strong and did a lot of the lifting. Still I don't think he was used to hard work as he was pretty well all in by the time we were ready to go.

After I got settled and got the routine down, I had more time on my hands. I would check the cattle and the pastures as I put out salt. Most of the pasture had a natural barrier but there was a drift or line fence on the lower end. Somebody else was delegated to take care of that but I was kind of expected to keep an eye on it as much as I could. I believe they had a fence rider check it once in a while however.

I wasn't harnessed to any set schedule so I would do the riding when the weather was good. There was a certain amount of cold wet weather though and I spent those days in camp. After the newspapers arrived, I would pour through them but there wasn't enough reading there to occupy all my spare time. Then one day I remembered the Bible in my warbag. It was kind of strange that I had it along as I thought I had left everything in the pick-up that I absolutely wouldn't need. I had just overlooked taking it out.

It was a cold chilly day and a misty drizzly rain was falling. There was no point in riding as the visibility was very poor anyway so I stoked up the fire in the stove and lay back on the bunk after eating breakfast. My thoughts turned back to other days.

When Dad passed away, it was kind of sudden and when Mom got a hold of me he was already dead. She had called all the rodeo offices at places where I might be entered and finally got a hold of me. I was entered in a rodeo in Nebraska when I got word of mother. My sister Pearl was a little more sophisticated about communication and simply called the head Rodeo Association office and the secretary there put out the word and got a hold of me. I called and she told me mother had not been doing so well. Mom was not one to run to doctors much and when she finally went, she was diagnosed with cancer. She said she didn't have much time left. So I quit rodeoing for the time being and went home. It seems mother had gone in for what they thought would be a gall bladder operation but found her full of cancer when they opened her up. So it was only a matter of time. She was already on sedatives to kill the pain so it was hard to talk to her. There was nothing much they could do in the hospital so she came home for awhile.

One day as she lay in bed, I was sitting in the recliner beside her. I thought she was asleep but she suddenly said, "Will?"

"Yes mom."

"Will." Her words were soft and very slow.

"Yes mom."

"Will, I never gave you kids a very formal religious training. It seemed we were so busy making a living. I feel bad about that."

"You did a good job, Mother. Remember when you read us Bible stories?"

"I know. But I should have done more. Reach under the bed, Will. There is a box there. Bring it out."

I looked under the bed and beside her slippers was a small black box.

"Open it, Will."

I opened it and inside was the family Bible.

"Will, the other kids all have their family Bible. I gave them each one for their wedding present. I want you to have this one."

Her voice trailed off. I thought she was resting and was going to say more but she had fallen back to sleep. I reached over and kissed her forehead. My tears dropped on her cheeks. Those were the last words she spoke. She died that night.

I got out the Bible and thought if I were ever going to get acquainted with it, there would never be a better time. I read most of the day. It was hard reading and even harder to understand. By summer's end, I had read through once and then parts of it several times. There was sure a lot to ponder as I rode back and forth and all over the big pasture.

On the other side of the valley from Boulder Creek up in the mountains is a place called Crescent City. They have a big rodeo there every year towards the end of July.

Crescent City was originally a mining town but when the mines played out, it became pretty much a ghost town. There was some ranching around there and there were a few hangers on but eventually the town lost the post office and it got down to only a few people. There was a small grocery store that sold gas out front, a cafe and, of course, a bar. Then tourists discovered the beauty of the country up there and the place started to thrive again but only in the summer.

As an added attraction, the town's people had a little summer festival and to that was added a rodeo. The novelty of a rodeo way back up in the hills got more people to come and the thing got to snowballing 'til it was one big blow-out. I had heard of it when I was riding but never got there and when I quit competing, just kind of forgot about it.

Then in the papers Bill sent up I read an advertisement and write-up about the coming rodeo in Crescent City. I still didn't think much of it as I was kind of tied down here and keeping out of sight and enjoying myself. But when the camp tender came the next time, there was a note from Bill. I guess he figured I had everything under control and if I wanted a few days off, I could come into the ranch with the camp tender next trip. The ranch crew was going to take in the Crescent City Rodeo and I could go along or take my rig. When they got back, someone could drive me back to base camp and I would be back on the job. I don't know if this was Bill's or Gary's idea, but someone maybe thought a break would be good for my morale. I scratched out a reply that if I was going I would come down.

I thought about the trip 'out' for the whole two weeks. It would be fun to get back to a rodeo again and see who was there that I might know. On the other hand I really wouldn't be able to visit much if any because I would just as soon not have anybody know I was up here. And of course I was working under another name. I doubt that anyone would recognize me as I had quit shaving when I went up. All I would have to do would be to put on a pair of bib overalls and wear a cap and I doubt that anyone would recognize me. But then it wouldn't be much fun. Still the thought intrigued me.

I thought of Sandy. By some strange quirk of fate, would she be there? And if she were, would she be alone? These thoughts troubled me exceedingly. One day I would decide to go, the next I decided not to. I kept flip flopping on the idea. I made preparations to go even though I hadn't fully made up my mind. I put out salt to all the spots. Checked the stock. Everything was on go. Even the morning of the day the camp tender came, I packed a bag and brought it with me to base camp. There would be grass enough in the trap pasture for a week for the horses. But at the last minute, I decided not to go. I would be a stranger in a world that I had known so well. And if by chance, someone did recognize me, it might be very embarrassing.

CHAPTER 14

In talking to the camp tender, I learned that there was another pasture rider in the valley west of me. This was another community pasture and his camp would only be about fifteen miles from mine but up over the hump. I wondered if there was a trail over and where it was. I asked him to ask Bill about it. On the next trip, Bill sent a note with a map and there was a trail over but it was pretty rough. Mostly a game trail. It was on into August now and I thought maybe I would ride over one day, spend the night or more and then come back. It would be kind of nice to visit with someone with more my own interests for a change. The camp tender had run out of new ideas on the first trip.

So one bright morning, I saddled up, threw my bedroll on a pack horse along with some essentials and took off with Bill's map in my pocket. Fifteen miles ain't much in open country but in that rough mountain country it can be plenty. I had to stop a few times to cut blow down trees out of the way and things like that. At times, I wasn't sure I was on the right trail but I finally peaked out on the divide and the signs all fit. The view from up there was spectacular to say the least. I felt a little lonely though. Well not lonely as much as the desire to share this with someone. Or maybe that's what lonely is. It just didn't seem right for all that grandeur to be here and only me to see it.

I started down the other side, crossed a small valley and picked up the trail again going up. It was getting late and I was beginning to think I may have missed it when I smelled smoke. I urged the horse ahead up a winding trail and into a grove of trees where there was a corral and cabin. I observed the Code of the West as no one would be expecting me here. I yelled out, "Hello the camp." No one answered so I yelled again. Still no answer so I decided no one was home. I tied the horses and walked up to the cabin. I knocked again and was about to go in.

The Code of the West was also that if no one is home, make yourself at home. The party may be gone for a few days and a traveler was expected to help himself. He was also expected to leave the place like he found it. Especially to leave the wood box full so when the tenant came back he would have the makings of a fire. I had my hand on the latch and was about to enter when I heard the voice behind me.

"Looking for someone?" It was a gravely voice and not a bit friendly and it caught me by surprise. I spun around and was about to give him a piece of my mind but he was carrying a rifle and I didn't like the look in his eyes.

"How do you do? I'm Will Jameson and I'm riding pastures over the ridge. Thought I would come over for a visit." My mind was racing. I should have known someone was home or there wouldn't have been smoke coming out of the chimney.

He acted like he hadn't heard me and I was about to repeat myself when he said, "Put your horse up in the corral."

I unsaddled and the horses rolled. There was no feed in the corral and I noticed his horses were out in the trap pasture.

"Be okay to turn them out?" I asked.

He nodded and I opened the gate. Without being asked, I carried my bedroll to the cabin.

"I hate to be impolite but have you eaten? I am getting pretty gant. I just packed a cold lunch when I left this morning."

"I'll make supper." He replied gruffly.

He was still carrying that rifle and he, too, was carrying a hand gun. It looked like a 38 Cal. Smith and Wesson.

Much as I hated to, I thought I had better continue to observe the Code of the West and I unstrapped my .45 and hung it on the empty bunk. He seemed to relax a little after that and set the rifle down. But he never turned his back on me and he was still carrying a revolver. It was even a little amusing as he fried up some potatoes and meat and biscuits and coffee, as he had to kind of stand sideways most of the time. He lit a Coleman gas lantern and hung it over the end of the table.

All this time, he never said a word. When we finally sat down to eat, I had pretty well lost my appetite but tried to eat anyway since I had requested supper. If he had been observing the code, he would have asked me if I were hungry. As we sat down under the light, I had a good chance to really look over my host. He was about thirty years old, about 5'10" tall and a little stocky. He had black unruly hair and cold, dark eyes. Although he wasn't exactly growing a beard like I was, he wasn't exactly rushing a razor either, as he had about ten days' growth of black whiskers that didn't quite cover a long scar down the left side of his jaw.

About then I wished I had worn that 9mm under my shirt but that was back at home camp in my warbag. He had never volunteered his name. I tried to start a conversation several times with bland terms about the weather and stuff like that but all I got was grunts and nods in return. I finally gave up and tried to concentrate on eating.

I still had half a plate full of food when he was through. He got up and pointing to the empty bunk said, "You can sleep there." Then picking up the rifle, "I got to go check on the horses."

I had expected him to return but he never did. I would have been glad to wash the dishes but I didn't want to go poking around the cabin looking for stuff so I just waited. After awhile I rolled out my bedroll on the empty bunk and lay down. I pulled off my boots but didn't undress. I picked up my gun belt and placed it beside me and covered up with a blanket and held that old .45 in my hand under the blanket. When he came back in, I would pretend to be asleep.

I wondered what kind of whacko he was. Was he on the dodge or did he go crazy from being alone too long? Or was he crazy and this was the only kind of job he could get? And then I wondered if anybody had ever disappeared from these line camp jobs. There were a million places where you could get hurt and lost and nobody would ever find you. And if someone wanted to hide you, the odds were even better.

Along about midnight, the gas lantern ran out of fuel and slowly went out. There was no moon but the sky was full of stars and there was a pale light out as I could see through the two small windows of the shack, but inside was as dark as a coal bin. I kept hearing noises and was jumpy as hell. Finally I thought, hell if he wants to kill me, he could do it anytime and I wouldn't have a chance. I might as well get some sleep. But try as I might, I couldn't sleep. I thought I could hear footsteps all night, and of course the wind in the trees made all kinds of noises.

After a long, long night, it started to pale up with the dawn. With daylight, my thinking process started working a little better. I had to get philosophical about this. If he wanted to blow me away, he was holding all the aces. There were a hundred places to hide around here and he knew them all so I might just as well act like I didn't have a care in the world. I got up, strapped on my Colt and rolled my bed. When I opened the door would be his best chance though and I threw my bedroll out first as a decoy. When nothing happened, I stepped out on the porch. Picked up the bed and walked to the corral whistling the 'San Antone Rose.' I'll admit, my lips were pretty dry.

As casually as I could, I looked all around and didn't see a sign of him, although, I was sure I was being observed. I whistled up my horses and they came running. They thought I had grain for them and I sure hated to disappoint them but this time there was none. I saddled up and threw my bed on the pack horse. I was real tempted to check the 30-06 in the scabbard to see if the shells had been taken out but figured again that if he had wanted to do me in, he probably would have by now. I stepped up and slowly rode off down the trail.

The trail went for about two hundred yards and then there was a small rise. Then there was a slight dip and another fifty feet to an outcropping of rock from which I would disappear. I rode slowly trying to keep from spurring my horse to safety. The sweat started trickling down my back between my shoulder blades. I finally reached the rise and I thought now I can spur around the outcrop and be safe. Then I thought, what the hell? God hates a coward. I stopped and turned my horse sideways, looked back up the trail towards camp into what I was sure was the scope of a rifle, and gave him the finger.

I turned slowly around and walked the horse the last fifty feet to safety. I admit though that my shoulder blades were twitching 'til I rounded the bend. After rounding the bend, I put the spurs to Red and we started covering ground. After all, we weren't safe yet. He just might decide to follow me. Maybe he just didn't want any bodies around camp. He might decide to pick me off on one of those narrower trails, dump the body over the edge into a canyon and no one would ever know. The horses would go on back to camp and when anyone came looking, they would be looking in my pastures, not his. When I got far enough along, there were places I could observe the back trail. I pulled out the 30-06 (it was still loaded) and used the scope to scout the back trail but didn't see anything. Still he might know of a shortcut and be waiting ahead.

Then I got to thinking about last night. Maybe he had gone on ahead and was waiting to ambush me. But I saw only my own tracks coming in so kind of discounted that. Then maybe he wasn't even around. If he were on the dodge, he might have thought I was a law man and took off last night. He could have snuck a horse out away from camp and be long gone by now.

I finally reached the divide and although I felt pretty safe by now, I dismounted and led the horse over the top. I didn't want to make another perfect target on the skyline. I had lost my impulsive bravado from a few hours earlier. We made a lot better time going home as the trail was clear and the horses were heading back to camp. We got in about midafternoon and by now my appetite had returned threefold. I put the horses away, cooked up a big bait and stuffed myself. Then the combination easing of anxiety, the lack of sleep, and over-eating, overcame me and I rolled out the bedroll, lay down and died.

I don't know how long I slept but it was towards morning that I heard hoofbeats out in front of the cabin. I thought at first that a gate had opened and some of the horses had gotten out. Then I heard footsteps and the door slowly opened. There framed in the comparative light he stood with that rifle in his hand. He slowly raised the rifle and pointed it at me. I grabbed the .45 hanging on the peg by the bunk, swung it up and pulled the trigger but all I heard was a click. I eared the hammer back and fired again and again and again but each time I heard that click, click, click. Then he threw his head back and let out a loud coarse laugh and his face mysteriously lit up. IT WAS VITO MONTICELLO. Then I woke up.

I was sitting up in the bunk, my hands held out in front of me. Although it was dark, I knew they were empty. I was drenched with sweat although I felt a cold chill. When I had laid down, it was warm and I had left the door ajar. Now a cold night breeze had come up and blew the door open but no one was there.

I got up and carefully closed the door and latched it. I also pulled the latch string in. I laid down again but I knew there would be no more sleep for this night. The body was weary but my nerves were still wired. That was not to be the last nightmare I had that summer either.

Morning finally came. It always does. I got up and checked the yard but there were only the hoof prints of my own horses when we came back yesterday. I tried to put the past two days out of my mind and get on about my job but once again I was spending a lot of time looking over my shoulder and checking my back trail. Right about now I would have been happy to have a good watchdog companion but I didn't and would have to make the best of it. I was reasonably sure that the dude from over the divide wasn't going to come hunting me but the guy was obviously a little squirrley and you just never know what a guy is going to do who is a few quarts low on the dipstick. All I know for sure was that he had kind of ruined the rest of my summer.

I was really getting to enjoy my occupation. I missed the excitement, friendship and camaraderie of rodeo but after the 'incident', I didn't feel like I had better be around for awhile. And if I hadn't ended up in this camp with its great surrounding beauty daily proclaiming the glory of God, I might never have sought out the truth of his word.

I was due to go to the base camp in a few days and I considered sending word to Bill concerning what happened but the more I thought about it, the more I decided to let it pass. The guy may be wanted by the law and they would probably send someone up here to question me. I was here under an alias and trying to keep a low profile so I let it go.

I took a few precautions around camp. I strung a line across the trail to the shack each night just at dark. It was about knee high and I hung a bunch of cans and junk on it. No one would sneak in on me in the dark. I also latched the door each night and pulled the latch string in. Still if a professional assassin was out to get me, I wouldn't have a chance. It would have been a routine job for Tom Horn.

The days and nights were getting cooler and the leaves were starting to turn. The mountain meadows were putting on their fall colors and dressing up in all their majesty as if preparing for one big party before winter set in. And then one morning I looked up and saw the top of the mountain covered with snow.

When I went down to base camp the first of October, Bill was there to meet me. The kid had gone back to college. Bill had come in early and had the coffee pot on and a lunch ready. He lay out the plans for the next two weeks. We would be rounding up the middle of the month. There would be no salt to pack back this time. I would be taking in some camp gear. There were two big tents and all that goes with it. I was to have the tents up and firewood cut and things like that. On the 'day' about twenty cowboys would ride up and comb the pasture. It took two days and the crew would stay overnight once. He was even sending a cook. On day two, everyone would help tear down camp and the cook would bring the pack string back to base camp. The roundup crew would push all the cattle into the trap pasture at base camp. The next day they would be trailed about fifteen miles to a ranch that had a good set of pens and working corrals where all the herd would be sorted and trailed home to the various owners.

It was a reversal of the spring drive although the crew that rounded up were all pretty much 'hands'. The weather was crisp and cold but by midday had warmed up considerably and heavy jackets that felt thin in the morning were tied behind the cantel in the afternoon. Most of the cattle had already moved to the lower end of the pasture but we still had to comb the whole pasture to be sure there were none missed. The cattle were moved out and after the first snow, someone would ride the pasture one more time to see if anything had been missed.

The overnight camp was one of storytelling of the day's events and of other roundups of other times and places, and then eventually the fire burned low and the tired hands turned in. All too soon the cook banged on a dishpan and yelled, "Come and get it."

The hands turned out and filed into the cook tent. The cook had stacks of golden hot cakes and a big pan of scrambled eggs mixed with chunks of ham. It was sure a treat to eat someone else's cooking for a change. We downed several gallons of hot coffee and then it was time to saddle up. A wrangler had jingled the horses up into the corral and we saddled up just as it was paling in the east. We then tore down the camp and packed all the gear and started the cook off with the pack string. Then it was everyone mounting up and making the last circle.

We pushed the last herd into the holding pasture at sunset. The base camp looked like a small city. The two big tents were pitched for the crew as expected, but there were a number of pick-ups and trucks and several other tents pitched as well. A number of people, men, women and children had come up to 'help' trail the cows home. Many had ridden their horses from the last ranch, as the road into base camp was not really good enough to pull a trailer in.

The feed in the cook tent was a real feast that night. Many of the ranch women had brought in extra goodies and I ate 'til I hurt. I found my bedroll and gear and by helping the cook clean up, got to roll it out in the cook tent.

The next morning was an epic of organized confusion. The cook was up first to start breakfast and of course he is king in the cook tent. I rolled my bed and gave him a hand which was just fine and still according to the Code of the West. However, it wasn't long before several of the women came to help out and it got to be a case of trying to keep out of each other's way. The cook was getting pretty perturbed but breakfast was finally on and everyone dove in. Besides the hands, neighbors, ranchers and families there were also a few paying dudes along this trip.

The sun didn't come up this morning. It was a dull overcast day with a cold chilly wind that was going to be in our face all the way. We got the herd strung out and about midmorning, a few snowflakes started hitting us in the face. Looking back, we could see the mountains were being hit with a storm. Got out just in time.

Except for the cold wind and having to push the cows against it, it was an easy day. We got in early and put the herd in a trap pasture. Camp was set up in one of the big sheds so everyone was out of the weather. The cook was set up in the ranch shop. It was all cleaned up and tools put in all the right places. Probably the only time the place was cleaned up all year. The work bench was cleaned and a neat white roll of freezer paper lay down on the whole length of it. A big fifty-cup coffee maker was plugged in. Also in evidence were electric roasters full of tantalizing dishes. On the end was a big dishpan full of a mixed salad. Hey, the west had come a long way from the old chuck wagon with beef, biscuits and beans. The feast that night was even better than the last and I was sure I was going to founder.

Gary showed up for this wearing a spotless silver belly Stetson. He came over and shook hands and paid his compliments. He seemed rather cool and reserved but I didn't give it much thought at the time.

There was a big double barrel stove at the end of the shop spewing out warmth and though it wasn't as aesthetic, it sure beat a camp fire for being practical. It was another raw, cold day and after breakfast everyone turned to. There wasn't room in the corrals for the whole herd so a bunch was cut off and run in and sorted and then another bunch. The various herds were held separate off at a distance 'til the sorting was all done and then the hands from various ranches started pushing their herds home.

Although my job was officially done, I helped Bill and Slim push their bunch home. Slim's wife was also riding and even Gary and his son Boyd were there to ride along. The cattle weren't hard to move. They remembered the trail from one year to the next and seemed to know there is rest and feed at the end of the trail.

I expect if they were caught in a storm and had the wind to their back, most of them would make it home on their own if all the gates were open. We turned them into a pasture on the south end of the ranch where there would be feed 'til winter set in and then rode on in to headquarters. It was a small pasture that could be rounded up earlier and cattle would be sorted off for market and the rest would be easily moved to headquarters for winter feed. Slim's wife had made up a big hot dish ahead of time for when we arrived and had it in the fridge. She went on into the house and put it in the oven while we unsaddled and put the horses away.

It was good to get inside away from the cold. As we warmed up and relaxed, the hunger started to gnaw at my stomach, as we hadn't eaten since early morning. Gwen had poured out hot coffee for us as we sat around conversing and waiting for supper. Gary and Boyd had come along in. Boyd was rather reserved and although he had been raised on a ranch, he looked out of place here. More like a dude from back east out west to play cowboy.

I was feeling weak when Gwen yelled come and get it. She set the whole roaster in the center of the table. It contained her recipe of 'Texas Hash' made up of hamburger, rice, tomatoes, onions and chilies. It sure hit the spot.

We retired into the easy chairs and continued drinking hot coffee. Gary and Bill talked some about the market and things like that. The warmth and indulgence of food made me sleepy and I was dozing off. Then Gary got up, slapped me on the leg and said, "Drop by my office in town tomorrow morning and we will settle up."

In the morning, I had breakfast at Slims' and then loaded up my gear in the pick-up. The battery was dead from sitting all summer and Bill had to give me a pull to get it going. It is not good for a rig to sit without running for a long time and I probably should have given Bill the key and told him to start it up once in awhile but I hadn't. In fact, I had wondered whether I should buy a vehicle at all when I purchased the pick-up as it was one way of tracing me through vehicle registration. If the law had been after me, I guess I wouldn't have but if I didn't have wheels, I would be dependent on public transportation and in all I figured I could be out of sight more with my own rig.

I drove into Boulder Creek and stopped in front of the office where Gary held court. He welcomed me in and told me to sit down. He had a big checkbook set out on the desk in front of him with the amount made out but no name written in. "Now if you will give me your name, I can finish writing out this check."

This one took me by surprise and as evenly as I could, I replied, "I gave you my name last spring. Will Jameson."

"I'm sorry sir, but we ran that name through with the social security number you gave us and they don't match. There is no Will Jameson."

A cold sweat started to form on my forehead. Was he going to run a con on me to keep me from collecting my summers wages? I was beginning to wish I had that 9 Mil. on under my shirt again. Then again, I was glad I didn't for I might have done something rash.

Then in a condescending voice, he said again, "Now if you will tell us your real name, I will finish this check."

Well I thought. I will be leaving this town anyway so it won't make any difference now. I looked him right in the eye and said, "William J. Compton. 474-26-5540."

His attitude changed abruptly. As he was filling out the name on the check, he said, as much to himself as to me, "Compton? Compton? Compton?" Finally. "You related to Buck Compton, the bronc rider?"

"I guess he's a shirt-tail relative."

"Well, here you are Mr. Compton." As he handed the check over to me. "By the way, we are very satisfied with your performance in the big pasture. You may not have been aware but you weren't quite as alone as you may have thought. The government men rode through several times checking on the grass and range and were very satisfied. It isn't often we please those people. And the cattlemen and ranchers are pleased with your performance, too. Our cattle are in good shape and our loss this summer is less than any season since we started the pool. If you want your job back next spring, just let me know anytime and it will be waiting for you. And by the way, we won't ask too many questions." He winked as he made the last remark.

I got up and left with my head kind of spinning. This guy was a cool one. Then I got to wondering if he knew who I was all along. He could have gotten the license number from the pick-up and run a check on it and then probably checked with the law to see if I was wanted. Not finding anything, he probably thought I was dodging a paternity suit or something. And then the low blow about government men. Why hadn't he told me about that in the spring? I done away with a few predators up there thinking there wasn't anyone within miles and I guess I was lucky that at the time, there weren't.

Well that was behind me now. I had a check in my pocket for the summer. I hadn't drawn a nickel all summer so I was feeling pretty flush. I went to the bank and cashed it. Actually cashed it for a cashier's check and some traveling money. Then I walked up to the Long Horn Bar to see if John D. McCormick was still there. He would want to know how the summer went and it would be good to talk about old times again.

I walked in but a stranger was tending bar. After the usual formalities, I asked about John D.

"I'm sorry." He said. "John passed away this summer. Apparent heart attack. He was found dead in his bathroom one morning."

I mumbled, "I'm sorry to hear that," and slowly walked outside into the cool sunshine. Damn, what a bummer. I needed some work done on my teeth and I thought this would be a good time to get it done. I had a few bucks and time on my hands. Among other things, I thought John D. could recommend a good dentist. Now it seemed there was nothing to hold me so I went to the pick-up and crawled in. I didn't know which way to go but the truck was headed south, so that's the way I went.

CHAPTER 15

As I drove slowly down the highway, a sensation slowly crawled over me and I began to feel terribly lonely. It's strange. I was alone all summer and though I could have enjoyed company from time to time, I wasn't really lonely. Perhaps I had the security of a job, the horses for companions, the shack for a home and was surrounded by beauty. Now I was back among people but that didn't seem to help. I didn't have any real close friends. My folks were dead and I had very little in common with the rest of the family. In fact, for all practical purposes, Buck Compton had disappeared from the face of the earth for several months and nobody noticed. A car roared by and honked his horn. I noticed I was over the center line. I realized I wasn't paying attention to my driving and a few miles up the road was a roadside park. I pulled in and parked.

I thought about John and wondered where he is now. I pushed into my warbag and pulled out the Bible my mother had given to me. I turned to the 23rd Psalm.

"The Lord is my shepherd, I shall not want. He leadeth me to lie beside the cool water."

I tried to shake it but a feeling of sad depression came over me. I was as adrift in the sea with nowhere to go and it didn't seem to matter which way I turned. I dwelled on the past. I could have had a ranch of my own by now and a family but it seemed I had nothing. I could begin to see how people turned to suicide when in fact they had so much left.

I finally got a grip on myself and got tough. "Hey Buck, get with it. You still have your health. Think of all the people in the world who would be glad to trade places with you. You have a pick-up, camp gear and clothes. Everything you need to get by in life. You even have some money in the bank. This is no time to be in the dumps. It's time to 'Cowboy Up.'

" I reached for the Bible again and randomly opened it, "For He so loved the World that He gave His only begotten Son."

Hey, that's it. I do have a friend. A friend who gave his life for me when I least deserved it.

I strolled back to the pick-up and headed back onto the highway. Suddenly the sun came out and it seemed like a whole new world.

I drove southeast and went to visit an old rodeo friend in Kansas. He had been a saddle bronc rider but now operated a saddle shop. I ended up helping out around the shop and bunking out in the back room. I stayed there long enough to get my teeth fixed and awhile besides, but it was a case of being indoors too much for me and I eventually drifted on.

The next few years, I drifted around doing any number of different jobs. I was mobile so I usually kept working at something. I even washed dishes for awhile. I had stopped at a truck stop for dinner and the place was kind of busy. There was some kind of commotion going on in the kitchen and someone was getting cussed out for not being there.

A middle aged woman came out and I jokingly said, "You looking for help?" She stopped quick and said, "You looking for a job?"

I thought, "What the hell have I got to lose?"

"Yes. Where do I start?"

I didn't even get to finish my dinner. She grabbed me by the arm and led me into the kitchen. There by the sink were stacks of pans and dishes. "Well, I thought, "let's get at it." And I tied in. After a couple of hours, I had the stack down to a manageable size. I asked, "Can I finish my dinner now?"

The woman, who was apparently the manager and who also did waitress work exclaimed, "Oh, I am sorry. I thought you were done. I didn't mean to interrupt your meal. Of course you can eat."

Once again, I had a place to bunk. It was a truck stop, cafe and motel complex. I had a room, three squares a day, all the dishes I wanted to wash and they gave me a few bucks besides. Washing dishes wasn't exactly a mind taxing job and my thoughts would wander as I put in time at the sink.

It was strange, as I went down the road on the rodeo trail, I was quite often near broke, and sometimes hungry as well. Slept in a car or vehicle many a time. Now I had a good place to sleep, plenty to eat and even though I wasn't getting high-paying jobs, was actually gaining on the bank account. But there isn't much glory to being a 'pearl diver.' It seems the regular dish washer was an alcoholic and he had went on one of his benders when I dropped by. When he sobered up, I was on the job and he got canned. I wasn't aware of all this and when I found out about it, I told the boss I would sure be glad to give the fellow his job back.

The boss lady said, "He'll be back again. Would you stay 'til then? It will make him a little more humble and easier to get along with, but don't suppose it will cure him." And that's the way it happened and I was on the road again.

During those years when I was drifting, I would get to reflecting on the past, especially when I was driving. I would get to thinking about rodeos I had been to and the incidents that had occurred.

After the years flowed by, I wouldn't remember too much about most of them unless something spectacular happened or I had made a big win or something but still it's funny that a lot of the memories are about little things that we wonder why we remember them at all.

It was when I was rodeoing back east that I was working for a contractor as a pick-up man for awhile. The contractor had hired a new announcer for this particular rodeo. I don't remember the details as to why the regular one didn't or couldn't make it but the boss hired this young fellow for the job.

A number of clowns, announcers, etc. got their start this way by just being in the right place at the right time. If they blew it the first time, they probably never got a second chance. But every once in a while, one of them had a real talent and they were off and running.

I saw the boss and him talking before the first performance as I led my horse by, and kind of raised an eyebrow as I passed, but the boss kept a poker face. He was good looking, neat and trim with a businessman's coat and tie on, but his hat and boots were plumb western. I don't know what kind of credentials he had but we didn't have to worry as he had a good voice and seemed to do all right.

As the rodeo went along, he announced the contestants and explained a little about the events and if everything had gone all right, I would most likely had forgotten about him, but it was in the saddle bronc riding that he proved his worth. We had one horse left to turn out in chute number one. He was a big roan named 'Iron Jaw' and he was bad in the chutes. Just as the cowboy was about to set down on him, he reared up and went over backward. If the cowboy had got hurt, we would have just turned him out and that would have been the bronc riding for that perf but he managed to get clear and he was going down the road to another rodeo so he wanted to take him out right away. Well old 'Iron Jaw' was upside down in the chute and I knew this was going to take awhile. Here is where the clown earns his money as he will jump in with some jokes, antics, or whatever, but our clown was out back getting ready with an act. Well, the announcer can use a time like this to announce the sponsors, upcoming dates, the weather, and the pie social at the Methodist Church and he would be doing his job. Now, most cowboys get kind of immune to announcers unless they do something spectacular. Or stupid. At times like this, I have seen some put on music. On a rare occasion, there is dead silence 'til the action resumes. But this fellow went into a narration that had even me paying attention.

"Ladies and gentlemen, the sport of rodeo has its roots deep in history. The Spanish brought cattle and horses to the North American Continent and hundreds of years ago, most of the communities and cities of Mexico and Central America had fiestas and celebrations at least once a year. If they were in ranching country, there would quite often be some contests for the Vaqueros. These were usually roping events or tailing the bulls or events such as that. It was not 'til the cattle industry moved north into the high plains that rodeo, as we know it today, began to evolve.

"Many of the roundups would have a few hundred head of horses in the 'Remuda', 'Cavvy', horse band, or whatever it was called, depending upon what part of the country you were in. When you get that many horses together there are bound to be a few rank ones in the bunch. Some outfits had more 'broncs' than others. In fact, some outfits were known for their tough horses. Anyway, the rank horses were sorted out and put into what was called the 'rough string'. Some outfits had more than one. Then cowboys going down the road who considered themselves a better than average rider might hire out as a rough string rider. This job paid five, ten, fifteen dollars a month more than the average cowboy but it wasn't the extra money as much as it was the excitement, satisfaction and the prestige of being the rider of the rough string that made it worth all the hazards and risks.

"Each outfit had its 'rough string' rider and each outfit was equally proud of their own. When the roundups would converge, usually in the fall and the fall 'works' were done, the different outfits would get to bragging on their own riders and how do you find out who is the best? You stage a contest. Broncs were brought in and the riders would test their skills and of such was the saddle bronc riding event born.

"Once in awhile there were horses too tough for even the rough string, broncs that get to be almost unrideable. Did the rancher get rid of him? No, he quite often kept the horse up close to the ranch buildings, probably in the Wrangle Pasture. Then when a cowboy came along looking for a job as a rough string rider, the rancher would run in the bronc and test out the cowboy's abilities before putting him on the payroll. Sometimes there were broncs that were almost unrideable or at least 'hell to sit'. The bronc might get a reputation that reached far and wide. Local cowboys wouldn't try to ride him anymore.

"Then once in awhile a stranger passing through or perhaps someone from a distance who had heard of the horse, would make a trip to the ranch to try his luck. Perhaps the stranger dropped into town and over a few drinks in the local saloon allowed as how he could ride 'anything with hair on'. The locals would tell him 'that out at the Bar T was a horse named Slew Foot that NOBODY could ride.' From there arrangements were made for a match and the cowboy from Rattlesnake Gulch, Arizona was going to try and ride 'Slew Foot'. Word traveled fast on the frontier and the Moccasin Telegraph spread the news like lightning.

"People started to converge on the Bar T and if you were in a big balloon up in the sky, you would see people coming in from all directions to the Bar T and for miles around. Men would load their families with food and camping gear in wagons. There were buggies and buckboards and cowboys leading pack horses.

"When the owner of the Bar T saw all the people coming in, Western hospitality being what it was, he ordered a few hands to dig a barbecue pit. He told a few cowboys to go out and bring in a big fat steer to butcher for the barbecue. Well, those cowboys went out and figured it wasn't any harder to bring in a bunch than one and besides, then they might get to do a little jackpot steer roping so they drove in a small herd.

"By this time someone would surely have arrived that had a fiddle, mouth organ, or jews'-harp or maybe all three. Maybe the rancher was well-to-do enough to have a piano. They would probably sweep out the stable or maybe wet down a piece of the yard and pack dirt and then sweep it clean. Anyway, they would have a dance, hoedown, baile or whatever, again depending on the country you were in.

"Eventually that barbecued steer was done. The ladies had made fresh biscuits, pies and all kinds of goodies with a big pot of ranch coffee. All this time the stranger from Rattlesnake Gulch was treated politely but with reservations as they didn't know yet whether he was a sure enough bronc rider or just 'long on brag'. The young girls and maidens cast shy sideways glances at him.

"After the feasting and dancing were done, there was a steer roping. Maybe the heavy end of the steers were sorted off and there was also a steer riding contest. But at last it was time for the main event and old 'Slew Foot' was led out. Most likely the rancher had a big round breaking corral and here the action took place. The bronc might be easy to handle and saddle, smart, saving all of his energy for the bucking off of this rider foolish enough to try. Or he might fight all the way and have to be fore-footed, snubbed-up to a big stout horse and blindfolded.

"However it happened, the cowboy was finally on board and he said, 'Turn him loose boys and let's see if this dude has any bucks in him.'

"And then the 'Ball' was on. However it ended, the rider and the rancher were sure to shake hands. If the cowboy rode him out, the rancher was sure to compliment him and tell him he had a job anytime he wanted on the payroll. If he bucked off, the rider would say, 'He was sure some bucker.' Even if he bucked off, the rancher still might want to hire him as it sure was no disgrace to buck off old Slew Foot and everyone could tell whether or not he was sure enough a hand by the way he handled himself and the way he rode. Everyone got a lot more congenial to the stranger and the girls and maidens added sly smiles to their glances.

"Of such things were legends made and stories, poems and songs were written about events like this such as the 'Strawberry Roan' and the 'Zebra Dunn'.

"And this is the heritage of rodeo such as you folks are seeing here today.

"And now I see that Harold Stern of Grassy Hill, North Dakota has his horse ready in chute number one."

With these words, he jolted one back to the present. I had been so engrossed in his little speech that I almost missed the chute boss's signal to go to the left side of the arena to get in position for old 'Iron Jaw'. I hadn't noticed the lapse in action and I doubt that anyone in the crowd did either.

If the boss had any misgivings about the young fellow when he hired him, he sure didn't now. He got more than his money's worth.

I don't know where the young man got all his knowledge. He might have come from a ranching background but he was more likely one of the new breed, a college cowboy and had read up on western history. I think he rodeoed with the N.I.R.A. (National Intercollegiate Rodeo Association). He did go on to become an announcer but eventually went on to other business and only announced occasionally.

Always there were the thoughts of what might have been. I still watched my back trail and tried not to be too visible but I figured I was safer now as time went by. Hell, maybe those people were all dead. Might have killed each other off. And Sandy crossed my mind continuously. Was she still alive? Was she well? Did she think of me?

Time kept moving on and the aches and pains were not getting better. It was in a town in Kansas that I had stopped for a meal. I usually ate in the working man's cafe where cowboys, ranchers and farmers would take their meals. I was just drifting. It was spring and I was heading north to get away from the heat. The place had the usual lunch counter and some chairs and tables. By the door was a big bulletin board with some auction bills tacked up. Also a few rodeo posters along with an assortment of 'for sale' signs and things like that. On the way out, I stopped to look things over, more to kill time than anything and there I saw the sign. 'Help Wanted. Universal Feed Lot.'

I thought, what the hell? and took down the number and address. I drove out and up to the office, talked to the manager and was hired. They needed, among other things, a night watchman. This was mostly a job of patrolling the pens to see that nothing was out of order. There really wasn't that much to do, it was just that if something went wrong like a water pipe breaking or something like that, there would be someone there to catch it. Also trucks would come in and unload or load up and I would check them in or out. There was a coffee maker in the check-in office and I was all set. Also, they fixed me up with a mobile home on the back side of the property in a small grove of trees so my room was taken care of. That was a good deal for them too as during the year, there would be heavy runs and then I would help during the day, too. They had saddle horses there for moving the stock so at times, I was back in the saddle again.

Although there were times that I could get pretty busy, there was a lot of solitude times. I started reading a lot and broke out that old family Bible and read it again. It was strange but some of those readings and gospels would have a whole different meaning when I read them the second or third time than when I read them the first time. I figured there had to be more explanations and I started going to church on Sunday to get another opinion. There were several churches in the town and I went to one and then another.

One Sunday I went to a Catholic Church. Mostly because I hit the place at the right time when I came to town. After the mass, Father Fitzgerald was greeting the 'sinners' as they left the church. I hung back to be last in line as there were some questions I wanted to ask him about the sermon and I didn't want to hold anybody up. I introduced myself and he recognized me for a new comer. We talked for awhile and then he asked if I had a family.

I told him I was a bachelor and he smiled and said, "This is the last mass. Why don't you join me for dinner? My feet are getting tired."

I smiled inwardly and accepted. I had sat down to table with all kinds of people in my life but a Catholic Priest was going to be a first. We walked to the Rectory. I guess I had expected a housekeeper but the good father was also a bachelor. As we entered I smelled the tantalizing odor of something bubbling on the stove.

"Irish Stew," the father said. "I get it ready the night before and put it on early Sunday morning. Just let it simmer and when I come in, dinner's ready."

The father was no slouch at cooking. The stew was delicious. This began the friendship of myself and Reverend Fitzgerald. He was from back east and knew religion but was also interested in the west and the cowboy way. I was from the west and knew that, but was also interested in religion. He had a great sense of humor and he got to coming out to the Feed Lot.

When things were slack, I would saddle up a couple of horses and we would go riding. He had never rode a horse before and for him it was quite an experience. He finally got the hang of it pretty good but never did look like a cowboy on a horse.

I stayed on here at the Feed Lot and I expect when and if I retired, I would probably have a part time job here. It's a place I can call home and this fall we are going into Colorado to go elk hunting. We will go up to where Doc Steen's ranch was. I know there will be mixed emotions about the trip.

I will be showing the Father the trail in the mountains and the 'Cowboy Way'. He has been showing me the trails of life that lead home.

I think I am getting a whole lot the best of the deal.